TRA

Slocum sli~~d~~ ~~h~~ol~~s~~ter and brought it forward, leveli~~ng~~ ~~o~~n the rock and aiming it directly at one of the men's heads.

"Sorry to break this up, boys," he announced in a booming voice.

Both Rome and London jolted to their feet, plates flying, their hands going for their guns.

"Wouldn't try that if I was you," Slocum said calmly, and they paused, mid-draw, blinking like owls in the light of a torch. "All I know is that you boys stole my horse and my belongings. Now, that sorta pissed me off, if'n you get my drift."

The two men below exchanged worried glances, but both their gun hands eased away from their holsters.

"That's it," Slocum continued. "Now, I don't rightly know which one'a you is which, but I'm willin' to wager I can nail you both before you can clear leather, and me and Mrs. Tanglewood can sort it out later."

"If you can sort her out, you're doin' better than me and half the folks in the county," the man with the scarless face said.

Tucked into the rocks below Slocum, the woman chuckled softly.

DON'T MISS THESE
ALL-ACTION WESTERN SERIES
FROM THE BERKLEY PUBLISHING GROUP

THE GUNSMITH by J. R. Roberts
Clint Adams was a legend among lawmen, outlaws, and ladies. They called him . . . the Gunsmith.

LONGARM by Tabor Evans
The popular long-running series about Deputy U.S. Marshal Long—his life, his loves, his fight for justice.

SLOCUM by Jake Logan
Today's longest-running action Western. John Slocum rides a deadly trail of hot blood and cold steel.

BUSHWHACKERS by B. J. Lanagan
An action-packed series by the creators of Longarm! The rousing adventures of the most brutal gang of cutthroats ever assembled—Quantrill's Raiders.

DIAMONDBACK by Guy Brewer
Dex Yancey is Diamondback, a Southern gentleman turned con man when his brother cheats him out of the family fortune. Ladies love him. Gamblers hate him. But nobody pulls one over on Dex . . .

WILDGUN by Jack Hanson
The blazing adventures of mountain man Will Barlow—from the creators of Longarm!

TEXAS TRACKER by Tom Calhoun
Meet J. T. Law: the most relentless—and dangerous—manhunter in all Texas. Where sheriffs and posses fail, he's the best man to bring in the most vicious outlaws—for a price.

JAKE LOGAN

SLOCUM AND THE RUNAWAY BRIDE

JOVE BOOKS, NEW YORK

THE BERKLEY PUBLISHING GROUP
Published by the Penguin Group
Penguin Group (USA) Inc.
375 Hudson Street, New York, New York 10014, USA
Penguin Group (Canada), 10 Alcorn Avenue, Toronto, Ontario M4V 3B2, Canada
(a division of Pearson Penguin Canada Inc.)
Penguin Books Ltd., 80 Strand, London WC2R 0RL, England
Penguin Group Ireland, 25 St. Stephen's Green, Dublin 2, Ireland (a division of Penguin Books Ltd.)
Penguin Group (Australia), 250 Camberwell Road, Camberwell, Victoria 3124, Australia
(a division of Pearson Australia Group Pty. Ltd.)
Penguin Books India Pvt. Ltd., 11 Community Centre, Panchsheel Park, New Delhi—110 017, India
Penguin Group (NZ), Cnr. Airborne and Rosedale Roads, Albany, Auckland 1310, New Zealand
(a division of Pearson New Zealand Ltd.)
Penguin Books (South Africa) (Pty.) Ltd., 24 Sturdee Avenue, Rosebank, Johannesburg 2196,
South Africa

Penguin Books Ltd., Registered Offices: 80 Strand, London WC2R 0RL, England

This is a work of fiction. Names, characters, places, and incidents either are the product of the author's imagination or are used fictitiously, and any resemblance to actual persons, living or dead, business establishments, events, or locales is entirely coincidental.

SLOCUM AND THE RUNAWAY BRIDE

A Jove Book / published by arrangement with the author

PRINTING HISTORY
Jove edition / March 2005

Copyright © 2005 by The Berkley Publishing Group.

ISBN: 0515-13899-1

JOVE®
Jove Books are published by The Berkley Publishing Group,
a division of Penguin Group (USA) Inc.,
375 Hudson Street, New York, New York 10014.
JOVE is a registered trademark of Penguin Group (USA) Inc.
The "J" design is a trademark belonging to Penguin Group (USA) Inc.

PRINTED IN THE UNITED STATES OF AMERICA

10 9 8 7 6 5 4 3 2 1

1

At a face-burning, wind-lashing gallop, Slocum wheeled his Appy up one side of the ravine and ducked low to avoid the slugs whizzing past his head.

If the truth were told, he hadn't expected the Parker brothers to turn around and come at him like this. But he was ready for them.

He hoped.

Suddenly, he reined his Appy hard to the right, toward the shelter of a jutting rock—and hauled back on the reins a half-second later. Quick as a barn cat after a mouse, he leapt from the horse's back while it was still sliding to a stop, then rolled up to the far side of the rock.

The Appy, Panther by name, scampered out of range at the same time that Slocum took aim and fired back down the draw.

It only took two shots. One for each brother.

They fell from their saddles: Leroy landing clean, and Bill dragging and bouncing from the stirrup for a few yards.

But they were both dead, and they both deserved it. And they were both about as smart as a couple of brain-addled prairie chickens, Slocum thought with a shake of his head.

He stood up as their horses passed below him at a lazy lope. "Panther, fetch," he called.

While his black and white, leopard-marked gelding set out after the fugitive mounts at a brisk trot, Slocum slowly walked down toward the bodies.

Bill came first. Bank robbery, murder, and many minor charges, too numerous to mention, lay at Slocum's feet. Bill had been convicted of two murders back up in Flagstaff and scheduled to hang, but he'd escaped, aided by his brother, Leroy.

Leroy, too, lay dead. The charges against him had been the same as those against his brother, Bill, except that Leroy had escaped arrest, trial, and sentence. And had then come in at the last second to break his brother out of the hoosegow.

The two had ridden away, leaving four more bodies in their wake. After a sheriff was killed, and then half a posse, the authorities, at their wits' end, had finally hired Slocum to get the job done. It was one that they were unable to do themselves, and one that Slocum was happy to take: The Parkers had done enough damage during their time that the reward for them was five thousand dollars a head, or ten thousand for both.

He nudged Leroy with the toe of his boot. The body limply gave to the pressure, then fell back.

Panther lazily returned, pushing the outlaws' horses before him. Slocum hadn't had Panther too long—less than six months, to be exact—and he had figured out in the first couple of days why his former owner had been so keen to sell.

The horse was a cutting fool. He'd cut cows, sheep, goats, dogs, or people—anything that was milling in a mob—and he'd retrieve strays all on his lonesome.

"A body'd think that was a real useful characteristic in a workin' animal," Slocum mused as he hoisted Leroy's body across his mount's saddle and proceeded to rope him into place.

"'Ceptin' you do it all the time, Panther," he muttered, "and with no warnin' whatsoever. You big ol' lunkhead."

Panther whiffled air through those big freckled nostrils, and gazed at him, calm and unconcerned.

"Everytime we pass a herd of anything, from cows to goats to prairie dogs," Slocum continued as he roped old Leroy in place, "you got to rush in and cut somethin' out of it. Now, that's a fine trait, but I can see where that'd be a real handicap to a man tryin' to do a job. It can get kind of unsettlin', you know?"

He reached under the belly of Leroy's horse to grab the rope he'd just dangled over Leroy himself, and continued addressing Panther. "Especially when a feller ain't ex-pectin' it. Especially when he's got no need for a goddamn pronghorn or coyote or wild burro right at that minute."

Panther paid no attention and started to graze on the sparse vegetation. Slocum snugged the last rope over Leroy, and proceeded to hoist the late Bill Parker over the saddle of his mount.

Now, Slocum wasn't particularly fond of hunting down men for money. He'd been hunted himself, and he knew that sometimes, charges could be unfounded.

But he'd seen Bill and Leroy shoot down two of those men himself, and to his mind, there was no question of in-nocence. They'd done the deeds, and now they had to pay for them.

It was a simple matter of letting the law take its due and proper course, and Slocum being an agent of the law.

Sort of sideways, that was.

"Bounty hunter" wasn't a title Slocum relished, and he'd be glad to get these bodies back to Flagstaff and turned in. He would be able to slip out of the bounty-hunter cloak as easily as he'd slipped into it, and he'd have ten thousand to boot.

Ten thousand dollars could buy a whole lot of fine ci-gars, good champagne, and all the loving a man could ever wish for.

He snugged up the last rope, picked up the Parker brothers' reins, and whistled for Panther.

The bank teller in Flagstaff counted out the last of the money—in gold coins and hundreds and fifties—and Slocum stuck the last of the bills in his silver money clip.

Even with the rest of the cash tucked into his pockets, that money clip was plain overloaded.

He tipped his hat to the teller, said, "Nice doin' business with you," and walked out into the afternoon sunshine.

It had been a week since he'd brought in the Parkers, and he was getting to know Flagstaff pretty well. More than he wanted to, anyhow. Additionally, he figured it was time to get ol' Panther out of that stable and on the trail again.

If Slocum had restless feet, Panther had hooves just as itchy.

He stopped by the hotel and picked up his bedroll and his saddlebags, and then collected Panther. He figured he'd head down to around Phoenix. He hadn't been there in a while, and there was a certain gal he'd like to drop in on: beautiful and buxom Rosie, at Stella's place.

For Slocum, it was more than reason enough.

Three days later, when he had Rosie weighing heavy on his mind and was riding into the high and beautiful red rock country about halfway to Phoenix, circling wide of Prescott on purpose—wanting no truck right at the moment with the Whiskey Row crowd—with most of his newly earned fortune tucked into his saddlebags, disaster struck.

All he remembered was that he'd been riding through a crisp, clear morning alongside a sun-dappled creek, when somebody leapt down from the rocks above. The bushwhacker had jumped right on top of him and slugged him over the head.

Hard.

The only thing he had to go on to identify the thief was that he'd worn black britches. Slocum had caught just a glimpse of the goddamn thief's thigh before he'd passed out.

And now, here it was, coming nightfall. His money was gone—at least, what was in his saddlebags—his horse was gone, and all his vittles and possessions along with it.

"Great," he muttered as he sat up and felt the back of his head. There was quite a goose egg. "Just perfect."

On the off chance that those owlhoots hadn't made off with Panther, he whistled loudly.

He was instantly sorry. His forehead was throbbing, and the high-pitched blast of air through his teeth nearly knocked his head off his shoulders.

Scowling, Slocum sighed.

No Panther.

He bet they'd rolled him, too, those bastards. He hadn't thought to check. Immediately, his hand dropped to his side, and what he found turned that scowl into the briefest of smiles.

Whoever had made off with everything else hadn't thought to take his guns. That was something, anyway. He patted his pocket, and said, "Well, I'll be goddamned!" when he found his money clip still there, too, and still fat with bills.

He figured that the sonofabitch had been too busy thumbing through his saddlebag cash to bother with small things like a couple of pistols. Or a knife, he thought, when he ran a thumb around inside his boot top and felt his blade resting there.

Goddamn idiot, Slocum thought, and crouched beside the stream.

As he scooped up a handful of water and splashed his face, his newly cleared head began calculating his next move.

A man didn't steal from John Slocum and get away with it.

A man didn't take John Slocum's money, and most of all, he didn't make off with Slocum's horse.

Not if he wanted to see old age and a rocking chair, that was.

Slowly, Slocum stood up. He glanced skyward. There was still some time to track them this afternoon. He had maybe three hours before it would be too dark to go any farther.

His head still throbbing, he set out on foot. He was hoping that the yahoo—actually, yahoos: there were several of them, by the tracks—who was riding Panther just happened to cross paths with a herd of real jumpy pronghorn.

But the strangest thing happened about five minutes later.

He discovered he was trailing three riders. Three sets of hoofprints, counting Panther's. And Panther was carrying weight, as well. Which meant two of them must have been riding double until they lucked on to him.

He'd followed the trail back into the trees about thirty yards when he found one of his canteens lying smack in the middle of the broken brush and bent weeds that marked their track.

He picked it up and looked at it. Scowling, he hung its loop over his shoulder and walked on. Had they dropped it? It seemed pretty strange that a rider would be that careless out here.

If you dropped a canteen, you'd surely notice it. Wouldn't you?

Then about another fifty yards farther along, he found a brown package. It looked familiar, and when he opened it, all he could do was shake his head. Why the hell would somebody drop his beef jerky?

It was Slocum's all right, wrapped in paper from the mercantile where he'd bought it, and the contents bore the imprint of Slocum's teeth, where he'd chewed off a hunk that morning.

They'd have had to dig down in his saddlebags to find it.

He paused long enough to take another bite of the newly found jerky before he started walking again.

He didn't know who was in front of him, but he was feeling a bit kinder toward at least one of them. At least, for the moment.

It looked like the horse thief was dropping crumbs for him.

But why?

2

Beth Tanglewood, riding behind the Grangers at the end of a rope, surreptitiously reached back once more into the Appy's saddlebags, and pulled out what turned out to be a thick roll of bills.

She gulped air in surprise, then hid her hands when Rome turned to look at her.

"What?" he demanded, his dark, scarred face glaring at her ominously.

By this time she should be used to it, she thought, but she still found herself wincing at the sheer ugliness of that scarred visage.

"N-nothing," she stuttered.

"Well, shut the hell up, then, missus!" Rome Granger said, and then turned, ignoring her again.

Beth let out a careful little sigh. Rome and London Granger, who had obviously been raised by optimistic parents, hadn't lived up to their worldly names. They were hired watchdogs and retrievers—in this case, hired by her so-called husband.

Damn Bass Tanglewood, anyway!

But they hadn't returned her to Bass yet, not by a long shot, and at the moment, there were more important things to consider. The wad of money she'd hastily slipped under her leg, for example.

Making sure that Rome and London had their eyes on the trail in front of them instead of on her, Beth freed the roll and stared at it. Whoever that man was back there, he'd been rich.

Frankly, at the time she'd been amazed that Rome and London hadn't gone through his pack roll, but she supposed they were happy just to have his horse and leave him for dead.

The Granger brothers might be the best trackers around, but when it came to anything else, they were about as smart as a bag full of bricks.

The horse she'd started out on, over in Gallup, had broken a leg three days back, and Rome had shot it.

She still felt awful about that.

Nearly as awful as she had felt about having to ride behind one or the other of the brothers, smelling their unwashed stench, putting up with those awful wads of tobacco they kept tucked against their gums; their spitting, their farting, their burping, their none-too-subtle innuendos, and well, just them.

Plus which, the three times—the three times she remembered, anyway—she had tried to slip off her horse and sneak off into the forest, unseen, they'd caught her within five minutes. Thirty seconds flat was their all-time record. Which was why she rode with her hands unbound, now. Tied or untied, they figured that they had her, and they were going to keep her.

If they managed to get her back to Bass, she had made an oath that she'd pull the shotgun down from over the fireplace and give Bass both barrels, then reload it and give Rome and London one each.

Men. They were all pigs.

But she was hoping they'd never get her home.

That man they'd stolen the horse from had been alive

when they left him. She was sure of it. She'd seen him move.

And she was hoping to Jesus that he still had his senses about him, and was finding the things as she dropped them. She also hoped that she was remembering to drop them. Bass always told her that she was crazy as a bedbug, and she was beginning to believe him. Time just went missing, somehow, and she didn't remember things.

But to her best recollection, she'd dropped water first, then food, then things like socks and matches and a sewing kit: whatever her hand happened to land on.

She stared down at her hands. She wouldn't drop this cash, though. Carefully, she reached back and rummaged for something else, then stuffed the cash into her back skirt pocket. She dropped a book instead.

She figured that she might be dropping clues for a very bad man to find. Out here, you never knew.

But she was willing to trade the three devils she knew—Rome and London Granger, and damn-his-black-heart Bass Tanglewood—for one that was, at least, a new acquaintance.

It was nearly dark, but Slocum was still moving through the woods, tracking the sonsofbitches who had stolen his horse.

And picking up bits and pieces of the contents of his saddlebags every fifty to a hundred yards or so.

He was running out of pockets, but he sure wasn't out of hope.

He'd been thinking as he walked. After all, there wasn't much else to do, and these three yahoos had left a clear trail behind them.

They must have thought he was dead. That's all he could figure, because they had taken no pains whatsoever to hide their tracks.

So he thought and thought as he made his way down

through the pines and toward the chaparral, tossing and turning different scenarios over in his head as he went. He had started out just plain mad, but now he was having doubts.

The way he figured it, whoever was riding Panther was leading him along. And that rider was probably a kid. At least, Panther wasn't leaving very deep hoof impressions, not compared to the other two horses.

A lightweight rider, in his book, equaled a youngster.

Which opened up a whole world of possibilities.

Why would a kid take up with a bunch of horse thieves, and then drop a trail of canteens and jerky and medicine and clothing to help lead the fellow who owned the horse straight to them?

That didn't work. No, this kid was with them against his will. Maybe kidnapped.

Maybe he'd had a horse, and something had happened to it. Maybe the other two had grown tired of toting him double.

Maybe, maybe, maybe.

On the whole, Slocum was no longer angry at Panther's rider. He wasn't quite certain about the circumstances of the theft, but those other two black-hearted bastards were going to have to find new holes to eat with, once he got hold of them.

Briefly, he stopped and stooped to pick up a brown paper–wrapped package. He knew what was inside. One last fresh pear of the three he'd bought back in town.

He unwrapped it, discarded the paper, took a bite, and trudged on.

His feet hurt like hell.

"Off your horse," Rome Granger said gruffly, and slapped Beth on the leg with his reins.

"Certainly," she said as she dismounted. "Sure. Right

away, your majesty." She tossed him the Appy's reins and marched over to a rock, where she sat down, arms folded.

"Snooty bitch," Rome grumbled. "Y'know, Bass didn't say nothin' against deliverin' you back with a couple'a bruises."

"Try it and die," she replied without looking at him.

"Har, har," brayed his brother, London. London actually looked a little like a mule, Beth thought. A really ugly one.

"Shut up, damnit," Rome snapped, and handed both mounts over to him. "Just mind your own beeswax and get these nags settled."

"Sure thing, Rome," London said, still smirking. He cast an appraising eye over the Appaloosa. "Didn't get much of a chance to look him over before. Nice piece of horseflesh."

"Just settle 'em, will you?"

Beth simply sat and watched while they made camp. She didn't help. She never had, not once since they had pulled her from the hotel in El Paso. At least, she didn't remember it. She'd gone all the way to Texas, and Bass's bullies still found her!

Just my luck, she thought.

At least Rome and London had posed no sexual threat. So far, at least. But she didn't think they'd do anything that would make Bass angry.

When Bass was angry, he wasn't the most pleasant person. Actually, when Bass was in his most jovial of moods, he wasn't exactly a picnic.

But she'd married him, hadn't she?

What an idiot!

Of course, she'd had it on good authority that he'd be dead inside six months. How could she have known that he'd not only stay alive, but get completely well? How could she have know that he'd find himself a doctor who could cut that damned spinal tumor out of him and leave him walking, to boot? And that her oh-so-kind-and-loving ministrations would actually work?

And she'd been . . . more *well* then. She was having a respite from these blackouts—at least, blackouts of any significance—and for the most part, time had been running in a relatively smooth line for her. Until recently, that was. Things were getting bumpier.

And so what she'd thought was a meal ticket for the rest of her life had turned out to be a giant millstone. She'd tried to run away before, but he—or rather, his blood-hounds—always found her and brought her back. This last time, she'd gone all the way to El Paso, Texas, though.

It was the farthest she'd ever gotten.

Despite the grisly thought of being dragged back home, she was proud of herself.

Today El Paso, next time New Orleans, she thought. That was, if there was a next time. Rome Granger had already told her she'd never get away again. He'd said he and London were tired of tracking her everywhere, and that Bass was tiring of sending them.

She imagined that eventually he'd chain her in her room for good.

And nobody would notice or care, let alone do anything about it. When you had as much money and power as Bass Tanglewood did, you could get away with any damned thing you wanted. Which was why she had married him, for his money—or rather, her hoped-for inheritance.

But when you were a man, that "anything" you were entitled to included beating your wife—oh, he would whip her and beat her all he wanted, the bastard, but at least he wouldn't stand for anyone else putting a mark on her. It also included using her in any bizarre fashion he pleased.

And Bass was one sick sonofabitch.

"You know," London said, intruding on her thoughts, "I believe I'll take this here spotted horse for myself. I like him fine."

"Ride your own nag, London," Rome replied. "You know Mr. Tanglewood'll want that gray replaced."

"That's right, London," Beth spoke up. "Smokey was one of his favorite horses, and you shot him."

"He had a busted leg!" London protested, fear flickering briefly over his features. He was afraid of Bass, too. They all were. But she thought she had at least a little of their respect, because she kept trying to get away from him.

"Yup, he did," Rome said, then quickly, flicked his eyes toward Beth.

Beth was feeling merciful at the moment, and said, "Yes, I suppose he did."

This evoked an audible sigh of relief from London, and a grudging—and fleeting—look of thanks from Rome.

Even though she felt hatred against these men, she felt somehow in league with them, too. They could no more escape Bass's grasp than she could.

London traipsed back with the coffeepot and the gear to cook dinner. Rome proceeded to round up enough brush to make them a fire.

"Didn't find no canteens on that Appy," London said to her. "No food, neither."

"I got hungry," she lied. "And when the canteens were empty, I threw them away." She crossed her arms over her chest and said, "You want to make something of it?"

He regarded her for a moment, indecision flickering over his features, then mumbled, "Nope." He concentrated on pouring water into the coffeepot.

Beth cast a surreptitious glance back at the tree line from where they had emerged. There surely hadn't been time for a man on foot—and probably injured—to catch up with them yet.

But she had hope.

She felt herself drifting away again, going to that other place about which she remembered nothing.

She took a hard grip on the rock, and thought, *Here it comes.* . . .

"Just what the hell do you think you're doing!" she roared suddenly, and scared London half to death, judging by the look on his face.

"Aw, crud," Rome muttered as he picked up a stick. "She's doin' it again."

3

By nine o'clock, Slocum was crouched in the tall brush at the edge of the woods. He could see his quarries' campfire flickering.

More important, he could just make out his horse's wild, ebony and white leopard markings through the gloom.

He could not, however, see any people.

As he'd trudged after them, his feet growing sorer by the second, he'd grown increasingly angry with whomever had snatched that kid. And increasingly pissed that they had stolen his horse and set him afoot.

Of course, that last part went without saying. When a man spent most of his life in a saddle, he got footsore awfully quick, and the muscles in his legs were trained to grip a horse, not walk for miles.

He crept a few feet closer.

The fire was still a good fifty yards away, but it was partially surrounded by boulders twice as big as a man. They were likely back behind them, but he'd have to assume they'd posted a lookout.

Just where that lookout was holed up was anybody's guess.

Slocum, whose eyes had long ago become accustomed to the dark, slowly scanned the surrounding area with his spyglass—one of the "crumbs" dropped by the kid.

There were no trees, save for a few saplings, encouraged by what had been a damp spring. Plenty of rocks and thin brush and prickly pear cactus—a few jumping cholla, too—but nothing big enough for a man to hide behind.

He moved a few yards closer, careful to make no sound. There was a slight breeze wafting over his face, and he was glad that he was downwind from Panther. It'd be just like that damned horse to catch his scent and let out a whinny.

Despite himself, he smiled. At least somebody would be glad to see him.

He hoped that the kid would be, too.

He suddenly found himself wishing for a herd of mule deer to come wandering up. Now wouldn't that just create hell in a handbasket, what with Panther taking off, trying to herd them, and those boys all rushing around, trying to figure out what the holy hell was going on?

His grin broadened at the thought.

Slowly, he began to move closer and closer to the fire and its sheltering rocks.

Wrapped tightly in her blanket with her knees tucked under her chin, Beth watched as Rome and London Granger argued over the last bit of fried ham.

They were really a couple of dolts, when you came right down to it.

"It's mine, I tell you," London was saying. "I seen you sneak that big piece. Least you can do is gimme that little one!"

"Did not!" Rome retorted cleverly. "Never did no such thing."

"Did too!"

"Did not!"

Beth closed her eyes and said, through clenched teeth,

"Why don't you just fry up some more ham? You've got plenty."

There was a long silence, and she opened her eyes to see Rome and London looking at each other quizzically.

"I do believe she's got somethin' there," Rome said, looking at her from the corner of his eye.

"Could be," London replied with a shrug. Then he looked straight at her and asked, "Is you regular again, ma'am?"

She frowned. "I'm certain I don't know what you mean."

"Aw, hell. I'll get it," Rome said as he stood up and dusted off his britches.

"Morons," Beth muttered beneath her breath. She might be crazy, but at least she wasn't stupid.

London's head whipped toward her. "You say somethin'?"

"Only that you were a couple of idiots."

"Yeah, yeah," he said, plainly bored. It didn't get a rise out of him though. She supposed she'd called the both of them far worse since they'd picked her up in Texas. She just wished she could remember.

She glanced over toward the horses and once again admired the Appaloosa that Rome and London had stolen that afternoon. Clear markings, wide-set, intelligent eyes; sound, straight legs, a well-muscled rump and plenty of bottom. . . . She'd bet he could spin on a five-cent nickel and give her four cents change.

If he was alive, that man they'd stolen the Appy from was tracking them. She was hoping so hard that she'd talked herself into believing it was a certainty. Except that they hadn't broken a walk but once all afternoon, that she recalled, and he still wasn't here.

If Rome had killed him . . .

No. That was impossible.

She'd seen Rome crack him over the head, but she was sure it hadn't been hard enough to kill him, despite what

the Granger brothers had thought. They were fools, anyway. And she'd seen him move just a bit as they were riding out, she knew it. She'd seen him twitch his leg and flick
his fingers.

No, he wasn't dead, he couldn't be. But what was taking
him so long? They had his horse, and they had his money. A
whole lot of money, it looked like. When she started going
through the other saddlebag, looking for things to drop,
she'd found a bag of gold coins, too. It wasn't lightweight,
and it presently resided in another pocket of her skirt.

She hadn't counted it out, though. Not without Rome or
London seeing, that was.

She knew the bag of gold was still in place, just from
the weight of it. Surreptitiously, she checked her pocket for
the lighter money roll, and sighed when it was still there.
She never could be sure of what she'd done, these days. . . .

"He sure did travel light," London said, and her eyes
flicked to him. He was going through the stranger's saddlebags, this time more than a cursory check. "Hell," he went
on, "didn't even carry no food that I can find. Must not
have been travelin' very far is all I can figger. Either that, or
Mrs. Tanglewood, there, had a spell and dumped 'em out
for spite."

Suddenly, Beth was very glad that she'd stuffed all that
money in her pockets.

"London, will you just get that goddamned ham?" Rome
roared.

London dropped the saddlebags and said, "Hold your
goddamned water. I'm comin'."

He grabbed the last of the ham out of Rome's vittles bag
and made his way over to the fire. He tossed Rome the
ham, and as he sat down, said, "Feller didn't even have no
water on him. Don't that seem strange?"

"No water?" Rome asked, one eyebrow lifted.

"London, I told you," Beth interjected, and tried to appear bored. "I drank it, and I threw the canteens away. Cou-

ple less things to be clanking against my saddle and banging my legs black and blue. You boys got a problem with that?"

London looked at the fire, and Rome said, "I . . . I suppose not."

The image of Bass Tanglewood—and his imagined rage over their wasting time over such small things as a couple of canteens—loomed over them, she imagined. At least Bass—or more rightly, Bass's temper—was good for something.

It wouldn't be very good for her when she got back, though.

Bass would beat her, of course. He always beat her when she came back. And she supposed that she'd be held a prisoner in her bedroom, tied naked to the bedpost for at least three days. For most of which, thank God, she'd be off somewhere in her mind. That was par for the course, too.

But the things he'd do to her . . .

For a moment, she felt physically ill, but then got control of herself again—at least, as much control as she ever had, these days. She wasn't back home yet. And she was staking everything on a stranger who might or might not be dead.

Slocum crept up carefully, skirting the fire and going around, behind the rocks. And as he made his way silently up the slope of the rocks, so as to have the advantage of height, he suddenly realized that these men did not have a child with them.

It was a woman.

A woman with a soft creamy voice. A woman who called them both idiots. A woman who sounded as if she didn't wish to be in their company one second longer than absolutely necessary.

But still, it sounded like those fellows were kowtowing to her. She must be somebody important. And he wasn't entirely sure, from the sound of the conversation, that she wasn't actually in charge.

But then, why would she have dropped his belongings like so many crumbs?

It was a puzzlement.

And right at the moment, the main thing on his mind was retrieving Panther.

And his money, of course.

So up he went, inch by silent inch, until he could just peek over the crest of the boulders.

"Good ham," said a male voice.

"Yup," said a second. Then, "You're sure calm for a gal who's gonna get the holy hell whomped outta her when we get back."

Silence.

The second voice said, "Why come you ain't tried to run off on us again?"

The woman spoke softly. "Why bother, Rome? You and London always catch me."

The second voice, obviously Rome's, laughed and said, "You got that right, Mrs. Tanglewood."

The first voice, probably London, joined in. "We surely do, we surely do. We always get our man. Or woman. Whoever she'd decided to be at that there moment, and wherever she'd decided to take off to."

Tanglewood. Slocum hung motionless on the rock. Where had he heard that name before?

But he realized that his present position was not one in which to idly mull over such things, and made himself move again. Two feet of inching forward, and he could see down, past the rocks.

The woman, who must be Mrs. Tanglewood, was directly below him. Rome and London were sitting out a little farther, across the fire, concentrating on a few scraps of ham. One, he noticed, had a long facial scar, which had not been tended to, and had healed badly. Probably left over from a jagged knife wound, or maybe a tangle with some clawed animal.

Soundlessly, Slocum slid his Colt from its holster and brought it forward, leveling it on the rock and aiming it directly at one of the men's heads.

"Sorry to break this up, boys," he announced in a booming voice.

Both Rome and London jolted to their feet, plates flying, their hands going for their guns.

"Wouldn't try that if I was you," Slocum said calmly, and they paused, mid-draw, blinking like owls in the light of a torch. "All I know is that you boys stole my horse and my belongings. Now, that sorta pissed me off, if'n you get my drift."

The two men below exchanged worried glances, but both their gun hands eased away from their holsters.

"That's it," Slocum continued. "Now, I don't rightly know which one'a you is which, but I'm willin' to wager I can nail you both before you can clear leather, and me and Mrs. Tanglewood can sort it out later."

"If you can sort her out, you're doin' better than me and half the folks in the county," the man with the scarless face said.

Tucked into the rocks below Slocum, the woman chuckled softly.

4

There wasn't much left to eat, but Slocum made do with the leftover ham and some pickled eggs he found in the Grangers' saddlebags. He'd tied them up—the Grangers, that was—back to back, and now sipped at his coffee.

"So, you do this all the time?" he asked Beth. "Run off, I mean."

She regarded him almost primly. "Every chance I get, Mr. Slocum."

"It's just Slocum, no Mister to it."

He found himself staring at her over the rim of his coffee mug, and he liked what he saw. She was an unexpected beauty: dark, sleek hair, pulled back into a horse tail at the nape of her neck; large, clear, dark eyes, the color of coffee, and thickly framed in long, sooty lashes; lightly tanned skin with a soft scatter of freckles across her pert nose; plump, rosebud lips, teeth like the whitest pearls, and a figure that would make Lily Langtree jealous.

At least, from what he had seen. She hadn't risen since he'd arrived.

She seemed more leery than anything else.

"I heard them call you Mrs. Tanglewood, ma'am?" he said. It seemed she didn't speak until spoken to.

"That's correct."

"Ma'am, if you're wantin' me to help you—which I figure you do, since you dropped half the stuff outta my saddlebags to lead me along—you gotta tell me something about what's goin' on here."

Rome—or maybe it was London—snorted behind his gag, but Slocum ignored him.

"Where you from, for instance, and who's Mr. Tanglewood? Who are these two yahoos that stole my horse? What's the story?"

She stared at him for a long time before she said, "First, I think you should tell me who you are. Besides Just-Slocum-No-Mister-To-It."

He grinned. "Fair enough. I was on my way down from Flagstaff. Goin' to down around Phoenix. And I'd like my money back."

This time, she flushed. And rather prettily, he thought. At last, she stood up and fished around in her too-big pockets for the gold, then the folding money, and presented each one to him in turn.

"I assure you, it's all there," she said.

He just caught a glimpse of a tiny waist, a lush bosom, and bell-shaped hips before she sat down again.

"Bounty hunter, are you?" she asked, one brow arched. She didn't appear to like bounty hunters very much. Well, who did? And damn her for guessing it so quickly!

"Just this once," he lied, because he'd hunted for men before. "The law had about given up on the fellers I brought in. I saw a couple of their killings with my own eyes."

"So, you volunteered."

"Guess you could say that," he said, nodding. "The law was sure as useless as tits on a boar hog."

She lifted both brows in disapproval, and he added, "Sorry."

He couldn't tell by her expression whether his apology

had helped or hurt, so he said, "So, who's Mr. Tangle-wood? I'm assumin' there is one, and that he wants you back pretty bad."

"You still haven't told me who you are, Slocum."

He let out a sigh. She was making him work way too hard for it. But he said, "Not much to tell. I'm from the South, originally. Been out West since after the War." He tried a smile. "Guess you could say I'm a professional saddle tramp."

From behind his gag, Rome Granger snorted loudly. Slocum ignored him, but Beth had other ideas. She stood up, strode quickly over to where the Granger brothers were hog-tied, and pulled down Rome's gag.

"What?" she demanded.

"He's a killer, Missus. He's John Slocum! Why, he's known all over these parts, and . . ."

She put a finger to her lips and shushed him, then pulled his gag back up again. She turned back toward Slocum.

"A killer, eh?" she said flatly.

Slocum just plain didn't get her, but he nodded and said, "According to some folks. Other folks—the ones that aren't prejudiced by their professions—say I tend to be on the side of justice."

She came back to the campfire and sat down across from him. There was silence for a moment, and then she said, "We'll just see about that."

She thought she liked him. He was rough and wind-weathered, and his face, although not exactly handsome, had a rich and mysterious character to it. And he had followed her all the way out here, even if it was more to retrieve his horse than to help her.

But he had stayed on, once he'd made sure his horse was in good shape. It was something, though, his staying to help her. And he hadn't made one single move on her. Oh, she'd seen him looking, all right, but he hadn't done anything about it.

Admirable.

So she pushed aside her lingering doubts—after all, he hadn't murdered the Granger boys, had he?—and said, "Call me Beth."

A hint of a smile crossed his craggy features, and he nodded. "All right, then. Beth." And then he stopped, as if he was waiting for her to volunteer further information.

Well, she supposed she'd been snappish with him. And really, what could it hurt?

"Four years ago," she began slowly, "I married Bass Tanglewood. He seemed nice enough, and I had it on good authority that he wasn't well. His doctor told me that he was supposed to die within six months, as a matter of fact."

When Slocum lifted a brow, she quickly added, "I thought maybe I could help make the time he had left . . . easier. But then, instead of getting worse, he got better and better, and finally was restored to health once more."

She paused primly before adding, "The doctor said it was my doing. He couldn't think of any other reason."

Slocum said nothing but seemed interested, so she went on. She noticed that Rome and London had both turned toward her, too, like twin, trussed piglets.

"But when Bass got to feeling better, he got . . . mean. He took to beating me for no other reason than that he could. He did . . ." She stopped for a moment, not sure how much to tell, not sure how much she *could* tell, not sure how much she *wanted* to tell.

Slocum said softly, "He mistreat you? In the bedroom, I mean?"

Beth looked up sharply, but his expression wasn't lascivious, only kind and understanding.

She knew then that she'd been right to trust him. She nodded a "yes."

"Every time I try to get free of him, he sends these two bloodhounds after me," she said, nodding at the Granger brothers. "They may look dumber than dirt, but they always find me, always bring me back. And Bass always has a new, more cruel punishment. A 'deterrent,' he likes to call them. He is a beast, Slocum."

She took a long drink of coffee, then shook her head. "I don't understand. I don't understand how that sweet, bedridden, sick man could turn into such a monster. He was lovely, a true gentleman, when I first met him. Just lovely."

She stopped and let it rest there. She figured there was no reason to go into her former job at The Gold Star Dance Hall right now—if ever—and how she'd figured that Bass would die soon, and then all his wonderful, wonderful money would be hers.

The part she'd said about liking him back then, at first, had been true, though.

She really had. And she'd felt so sorry for him, too.

If only she'd known . . .

"Well," Slocum said after a thoughtful silence, "I reckon I can get you far enough away that he'll never find you."

She blinked. "You can?"

London Granger emitted an unbelieving grunt from behind his gag, immediately followed by a similar utterance from Rome.

Ignoring them, Slocum said, "How do you feel about Paris?"

"Paris, Texas, or Paris, France?" she asked, smiling slightly.

He returned the smile. "The French one."

"Why, I should feel quite fine about it!" she nearly shouted. "I don't speak any French, but I could learn, by jingo!"

"Bet you could," Slocum said, and stretched out on his blankets. He set his cup to the side after draining it, pulled his hat low over his eyes, and said, "We'll get started in the morning."

The Grangers were struggling in vain against their ropes more violently than they had since Slocum trussed them, but to no avail. Beth gave them a little salute before she, too, settled down into her blankets.

She was so proud of herself! She'd handled it quite well, she thought.

And she hadn't "gone away" for any of it.

Something—some little scuttle—woke Slocum in the middle of the night.

He kept still, slitting his eyes open, and peered across the dying fire at Beth Tanglewood. She was sound asleep.

The curious noise sounded again, and this time he recognized that it came from behind him.

Those blasted Granger boys!

He counted to three, then burst from his bedding, rolled to the side, and had his gun out before he stopped rotating.

There stood Rome Granger with London right beside him, and London looked like a fish pulled up on the dock.

"Close your mouth, London," Slocum said conversationally.

"I'll be danged," muttered London.

"Aw, shut up," Rome said, and elbowed him in the ribs.

"All right, boys," Slocum said, pulling himself up into a casual sit, but keeping his gun pointed directly at them. Or actually, more at Rome, who looked the most annoyed. "You know the drill, boys. Except this time, we're gonna tie all those knots just a little tighter. Got it?"

5

"What about them?" Beth asked, come morning. She and Slocum were mounted up and ready to go, and she was pointing at Rome and London.

Slocum shrugged. "They got loose before. They'll do it again before too long." He had mounted Beth on Rome's bay, a tidy little gelding with a snip and a star, and repacked his own saddlebags. He'd taken his good rifle back from London Granger, and it was safely tucked into its boot.

"Besides," he added, "I gave them a little help on the worst knots when you were . . . when you were back behind the rock." He almost flushed, but managed to hold it back, and changed the subject.

"Well, the quickest way from here to Paris is through San Francisco," he said loudly, reining Panther around. It felt good to be riding him again.

"You can catch a ship there that'll take you as far as China," he added, "maybe India. Or the train back across country, so you can sail from New York. Up to you. Now, let's get going."

Beth made a rather pretty little scowl of concern. "If you're sure they can work their way free?"

31

"I'm sure."

It seemed sort of odd that she'd be so concerned about Rome and London, but then, they'd been bringing her home for a long time, according to her. Maybe she had a soft spot for them.

Stranger things had happened, he guessed.

"Let's go," he said, and headed off into the northwest, with the lovely Beth Tanglewood riding the bay close on his heels.

But after they had gone five miles and come to a vast land paved with volcanic rock, as black and solid and rolling as if it had just cooled the night before, Slocum slowed, then came to a complete halt.

"If we're going to stop, couldn't it be in someplace with some shade?" Beth asked. It was the first time she'd spoken since they'd left camp.

Slocum dismounted and rifled around in his saddlebags. "Nope," he said, and pulled out a pair of nail snips.

"What are you doing?" Beth asked, as if he were half-mad.

"You might want to get down off that bay," was all he said. And then he proceeded to raise one of the Appy's front legs. He balanced it on his thigh, muttered, "Ho, son," and begin to snip off the nail heads that held the shoe in place.

There was silence for a moment as he worked, and then Beth said slowly, "I'm not going to Paris, am I?"

Having pried off the first shoe, Slocum moved to the next foot. "Nope," he said.

"Then where am I going?"

"Phoenix. Like I said, I was on my way down there, anyhow."

Snip went another nail head.

"But they'll find me!"

He looked up from his work. She stood ten feet away, her hands balled into fists, and man, did she look beautiful!

He had to work pretty hard to remind himself that she was another man's wife, even if she was trying like hell to get away from him.

With no expression, he said, "Not if they can't trail you, honey. It's a big country. I'm dropping you at Phoenix. Where you choose to go from there is up to you. I figure if I'm lucky, I might fox those Grangers as far as Frisco, which'll give you plenty of time to get to where you're really tryin' to go."

"Which is?"

"Honey, I've got no idea."

At his expansive home in southern California, just outside the ragged little town of Los Angeles, Bass Tanglewood sat uneasily on his front porch. It was wide and deep, and constructed in the Spanish style as was the rest of the house and the outbuildings.

It was, in fact, the old hacienda of some Spanish land grant recipient, who had long since been stripped of his house and his lands and his dignity, and been sent packing, back to Spain. Or maybe Mexico. Bass didn't care. He only knew that he liked the house, and the lands surrounding it.

Two small boys sat behind and to both sides of his wicker, high-backed chair. They fanned him lazily, using strings attached to their toes on one end. The other end was attached to Mexican palm fronds, hooked to the porch ceiling above him.

Bass was sipping at a tall glass of sangria. He fished out a slice of orange, pulled the meat from his teeth, and tossed the rind out into the yard. And he was thinking that this was what he was going to do to Beth when they brought her back.

Tear off her meat and throw the scraps in the yard. No, throw them to the hogs.

She deserved it. She was mad, and she was vulnerable. He would see that punishment was meted out. One attempt to escape her lawful husband, he would put up with. Even three, even five, by God. But this was the last straw.

The Grangers should be riding in with her late tomorrow afternoon. They had wired him from Prescott, as well as from Flagstaff and from Gallup and points all the way back to El Paso, where they had found the little harridan this time. They were good men. Good trackers, anyway. The best, even if they weren't the swiftest in the smarts department.

And his Beth? She was truly a little witch. Crazy enough to have wired him from that hotel in El Paso, asking how she got there, and was he angry? And then likely remembering none of it, not even the walk to the telegrapher's office. Mad as a hatter.

But she was the madwoman who excited him, who swelled him with passion, who inflamed his . . . baser instincts. He'd had others of course, but none fired him more than his Beth. Her cries and pleas, then maddened urgings for more, then anger and wrath—just thinking of them— had stiffened the front of his trousers as he sat there.

He made no move to shift his position. Who was there to see but a couple of Mexican brats, anyway? And if he felt anything, it was pride.

Not so long ago, he had not been expected to live.

His doctors had told him that if he did survive the surgery, he would never walk again, never sit up, never know the love of a woman.

Well, he had fooled them all, hadn't he? Beth had seen to that. Dear Beth, with her ministrations, her constant vigilance, her ever-present pleas and prayers and care.

Oh, he knew it was all for show. It had to be, didn't it? She was just a two-bit whore from The Gold Star Dance Hall—he'd had her investigated, by God, when she'd shown interest in a poor, lonely invalid seeing a specialist in New Orleans.

He knew all along that she was just waiting for him to

die so that all this could be hers: this California ranch, these vast land and cattle holdings, these vineyards, these orchards.

He also knew, all along, that she was a crazy little harridan. But a smart one.

When one is poor, one is simply crazy. When one is wealthy, one is eccentric, and to be tolerated. Perhaps she wished to be called "eccentric" instead of a candidate for the insane asylum. And his money would have done just that for her.

But he had astonished everyone. He would have made a very large wager that she was just as surprised as the doctors when he not only lived, but took his first faltering steps.

And she was the most surprised of all that first time he'd chained her to his bed, naked, and whipped and whipped and whipped her before he sodomized her. Even now, the remembrance of the horrified look on her pretty face—on all her pretty faces, or at least, those he had seen to date—still put a smile on his.

Well, on second thought, perhaps he would not kill her after all. Perhaps he would just make her wish she were dead. Her back, buttocks, and thighs were already covered with welts and scars, gifts from his whips and paddles. But her face? He had never touched that. It gave him such pleasure to look upon her.

But maybe this time he would purposely scar her, make her afraid to ever run again, make her afraid that her visage would make her a horror to all who looked upon her.

This was something worth considering.

"Miguelito," he said, as he stared out toward the mountains.

One of the small boys dropped his fan string, rose to his bare feet, and scampered to where Bass sat. "Senor?" he asked.

Bass handed over his now-empty glass, and the boy took it.

"More sangria, Miguel. Tell Maria to use more limes this time."

"Yes," the boy said, in concert with a small bow. "Right away, senor," he added, and ran toward the front door, the glass clutched carefully before him.

Having already picked up all the horseshoes and slid them into his and Beth's saddlebags, Slocum went carefully over the rock surface to find any nail head and bits of metal that he might have missed.

According to Beth, those Granger boys were damn fine trackers, and he didn't want to be undone by a single snip of metal shining on the ground. He cleaned away every trace of his having been there as carefully as if it were he doing the tracking.

Satisfied at last, he slid the bits of nail into his pocket, made sure every single shard and snip went in, dusted his hands on his britches, then picked up Panther's reins.

"C'mon," he said to Beth.

She started to mount up.

"No, on foot," he said. "Even without riders, these horses are already burdened enough with gear, especially barefoot and on solid rock."

He had expected a fight, but she didn't give him one. Instead, she simply nodded, and began to lead her horse after his.

He was going south, now. Not northeast, the way they'd made tracks earlier. He glanced behind him, and saw no trace of their having passed.

Good.

Beth led her horse up next to Panther, and he asked, "Where you from? I'm kinda confused on the accent. Some New Orleans, some Kentucky, a little California."

"Correct on all accounts," she said, staring straight ahead. "But you left out the six months I spent in Minnesota. And I was born in Illinois."

Slocum chuckled.

She looked over at him, her pretty brow hiked. She had brown eyes, as dark as coffee. "Well, I guess I wasn't in Minnesota long enough to pick up that funny Swedish accent."

Suddenly, the tiny silhouettes of first one pronghorn, then three, then five, appeared on the horizon. Slocum doubled Panther's reins around his fist and said, "Easy, boy, easy," as the gelding came to attention.

"What are you doing?" Beth asked.

"Tryin' to hang on to my horse," he muttered as Panther tossed his head, then bucked impatiently, lifting Slocum halfway out of his shoes.

Beth's brows knitted. "Huh?"

The pronghorn moved out of sight as swiftly as they had come and Slocum breathed a sigh of relief as Panther relaxed. A long chase after some damned pronghorn was the last thing he needed right now. But there was no need to trouble Beth with his cutting-horse woes. He said, "Sorry to make you walk."

"It's all right," she answered, and if she had any further curiosity about the odd little drama that had just transpired, she didn't remark on it.

"I've walked before," she said. "I've walked a good, long piece several times in my life, and it hasn't killed me yet."

"When?"

She looked at him as if she were amazed that he'd care, and then she said, "Walked all the way from Kentucky to New Orleans when I was fifteen. I walked halfway to Minnesota when I was eighteen. Caught a ride back down the river when I was nineteen. And then, when I married Bass Tanglewood, the bastard made me walk halfway across Arizona."

With that cryptic remark, she lapsed into silence.

Stunned wordless, so did Slocum.

6

London and Rome Granger worked their way free of the ropes by noon. Aside from a couple of chafed wrists, they were not much the worse for wear.

Except for London, who now found himself on foot, Rome having commandeered his mount.

It was now almost two thirty, and they had trailed Slocum and Mrs. Tanglewood—the damned, loony bitch, Rome thought—straight northeast. They now found themselves on a vast plain of nothing but sheeted and buckled volcanic rock.

Rome reined in the horse, and below him, he heard London mutter, "Thank you, Jesus."

"Don't go thankin' nobody just yet, London," Rome said. He took a long gulp from the canteen, then handed it down to London, who accepted it greedily.

"I know," London replied after he wiped his mouth on his sleeve. He started to hand the canteen back up, then thought better of it. He took one more swig before he handed it over. After another wipe of mouth on sleeve, he said, "Gonna be nigh on impossible to track 'em on this crud."

"That's puttin' it mildly, brother," Rome said, then stepped down off the horse.

London's face lit up. "My turn?"

Rome closed his eyes for a moment. "No, you idiot. We're both goin' shanks' mare. Gotta get close to the ground. I near bout lost 'em, except for that little scuff mark there." He pointed to the ground, and London followed his finger. "And start trackin' instead of watchin' your own feet."

"Steel on stone," London replied, nodding, and laid a finger alongside his nose. "I got you, Rome."

They began walking forward, noses practically on the ground, following a trail of tiny, nearly invisible scuff marks left by horseshoes on dark, volcanic rock.

They weren't some of the best trackers in the West for nothing.

"So, what you reckon he does, Rome?" London asked as he moved forward, eyes carefully scanning the territory ahead of him.

"Who?"

"You know. Mr. Tanglewood."

"When we take the Missus back, you mean?

London snorted. "Well, what'd you think I meant?"

"Don't know," said Rome, although he'd wondered the same thing. "Don't care, so long as he keeps bein' good for a regular paycheck."

Actually, that was partially a lie. Not the paycheck part, but the part about his not caring. He'd heard the Missus screaming up there, in her room. He figured about all the hands had, London included. And those screams sure weren't screams of joy.

They were downright terrible.

Except that they were broken by periods of laughter, crazy laughter.

If Mr. Tanglewood didn't pay so darned good, and if Rome wasn't sure that Tanglewood would hunt him down like a rabid dog and kill him, Rome would have gone up there and stopped it. Or at least, peeked to see what was happening.

But he hadn't, not once.

It grated on him a little bit, to tell the truth.

"I'll betcha he's beatin' her," London said. "Or somethin' worse."

"Yeah, probably."

"But it ain't our business, is it, Rome?" said London, in a rare philosophical mood. "I mean, he's the boss."

"He's practically the boss of the whole damn state, London," Rome said. Up ahead, he caught another glimpse of a steel scuff on rock. This wasn't going to be as difficult as he'd thought.

"Don't care about that," London went on. "All's I care about is he's the boss of *me* or not. And I reckon he is."

"London, you're a regular sage."

"What?"

"Never mind." Rome paused, then stopped and pushed back his hat. "What the hell?"

London looked around, but apparently came up empty. "What?"

"That son of a bitch!" Rome shouted, and beat a bony fist against his thigh.

Then it seemed to click for London, too. "Goddamn crafty bastard! He stopped right here and pulled their shoes! Goddamn it! I'm gettin' a whole new respect for him."

"Two people on two horses don't just start flying all of a goddamn sudden," Rome muttered. He tossed the horse's reins to London and got down on his hands and knees. He began gently sweeping the rock with his hands, moving outward in larger and larger circles.

"Ouch!" He pulled one hand back and sucked on his finger, then pulled it from his mouth. Embedded in it was a tiny splinter of metal. It was most likely from a horseshoe nail, considering the circumstances. Freshly cut, too.

"How we gonna find 'em now, Rome?" London asked, obviously worried about more than his job security. His own life, for instance.

Rome picked the nail splinter from his finger, gave it another suck, and testily, said, "Lemme stew on it a bit, London. Just shut up and lemme think."

Back at the site where the Grangers had camped the night before, a man knelt at their long dead fire, and looked over the signs that their struggle to free themselves had left on the desert floor.

At last, he rose and dusted his trousers with gloved hands. He turned to his companion, who was still mounted, and asked, "So, what do you think?"

"Looks to me like Slocum caught up with them polecats what took his horse, Harley," the mounted man said. He was the broader of the two, mustachioed, and spat a long stream of tobacco juice over to one side. "Figured he would."

"Think they got his money?" Harley asked. To Joe French, the mounted man, Harley was a fairly new acquaintance. He was lean, some might say skinny, with a hungry look about him. Joe preferred hungry partners. So long as they didn't get *too* hungry.

"Not hardly," Joe finally replied from atop his gray. "Man don't take Slocum's money and live too long. His horse, neither. Not unless they kill him all the way dead."

"Well, he let these yahoos live to rob somebody else, Joe," Harley said, and remounted his horse. "Looks like he trussed 'em good, though."

"Both of 'em done stupid things," Joe pronounced. "Dumb of them not to kill Slocum all the way when they jumped him back there." He poked a thumb behind them, toward the piney foothills, and the mountains beyond.

"Dumb of Slocum not to kill 'em when he caught up with 'em. The world's full of people doin' dumb things, Harley."

Then Joe pointed a black-shirted arm off toward the northeast. "Took one'a their horses to boot. And took one'a them hostage. Maybe."

"Maybe?"

"Mayhap it was a kid or a lady," Joe said thoughtfully, more to himself than Harley. "Lightweight, anyhow. Left 'em with only one horse between 'em."

"Who?" asked Harley, who seemed easily distracted. "Slocum and the kid or the other two?"

"The other two, you dolt," Joe grumbled. Harley had an appropriately hungry air about him, all right, but he was a little on the slow side. And it was beginning to grate on Joe.

Harley had come to him, up in Flagstaff, with this plan to follow Slocum and steal the reward money—an even split, fifty-fifty. Rumor was that Slocum was a hard case, Harley had said, and Joe had nodded as if he'd only heard the stories, too.

Never let on more than you have to. That was Joe's motto.

"See?" Joe added, arm outstretched, pointing closer. "Both of them fellers were tied up over there. You ever seen legs that long on a woman or a kid?"

Harley looked at the boot marks and the butt marks and said sheepishly, "Nope." He squinted ahead, his eyes onto the tracks leading away. "One on foot, one walking. They overlap the first two."

"Well, then," Joe said, and waited while Harley mounted his horse again. "You can be a real genius if you just try, Harley."

Harley's saddle leather squeaking, they moved out of the camp area, following the trail. "I sure hope so, Joe. I aim to get my hands on my half of that ten thousand and live like a king. A smart one, if'n I can."

"Hold that thought, Harley," Joe said with a straight face. "Just keep holding that thought."

And remember that it's one half, Harley, no matter whose idea this thing was in the first place, Joe thought. *One half and no more.*

Slocum and Beth, on foot, had covered the volcanic sheeting in a little more than an hour, and at the moment were stopped beside a rare spring in the desert.

Slocum filled the canteens to the brim, and the horses drank their fill, too.

"We can ride from here on out," he said as he rose from beside the little stream. He hung the dripping canteens from both horses' saddle horns, then turned toward Beth.

Seated on the ground beneath the meager shade of a palo verde, she made no sign that she'd heard him.

"Mrs. Tanglewood?" he said.

"I heard you, Slocum," she said, without looking up.

His brow furrowed. Here he'd foxed those boys who were hauling her back to her husband and was escorting her to the nearest safe stage stop, and she didn't seem to be appreciating the situation.

Shouldn't she, at least, be smiling?

"All right," he said, and squatted down beside her. "I give up. What the hell is wrong now?"

At last, she turned her face toward him. "Wrong?" she asked with that little brow raised. "Why should you think anything's wrong? I thought we were getting along quite famously."

Slocum felt his face screw up, but said nothing.

Women. He'd never understand them as long as he lived. This was 'getting along famously'? He could think of a few other ways of being sociable.

But he held his hand down to her. "Let's get moving."

She reached up and took it, rising in one smooth movement. "Thank you," she said, and walked to her horse, gathered the reins, and mounted—also very smoothly, Slocum noticed.

But that didn't explain why she ran so hot and cold, going from the grateful former hostage to this ice queen, and then to something . . . something he couldn't even put a label to. He shook his head and followed her to the horses.

"You're sure an odd one," he said as the saddle creaked under his weight. He backed Panther away from the stream.

"Who?" Beth asked. "Me?"

"Well, I suppose I could just as well be talkin' to my horse, here, but yes, you."

Her facial expression suddenly went from one of cool inquiry to that of a woman who'd just been asked if she wouldn't mind carrying a live badger in her underwear, and Slocum made the mistake of snorting out a laugh.

The expression quickly changed to one of embarrassment, then anger. "Are you laughing at me?" she demanded in a sudden vitriolic explosion. "You men! You're all alike under the skin!"

Slocum's "Hey!" went unnoticed as she suddenly lashed at her horse and galloped away, to the south.

7

It felt strangely good to gallop. The pins loosened in her hair, some fell out, and she felt her hair begin to billow out behind her.

Death to all the men in the world! she wanted to scream. Death to them and their ownership of all things, including women! Death to them and their ways!

And damn that Slocum! She'd thought he might be different. But no, he'd laughed at her. Laughed with that superior male snicker. She knew it when she heard it. She'd been hearing it all her life.

Hearing from the patrons when she was working, hearing it from her husband when he beat her and even when he wasn't, as if she were a dog that he could seek amusement from—and kick when he wished.

She heard Slocum riding up behind her, but she paid him no mind. She only felt the freedom of the wind in her hair, and the hatred in her veins slowly, surprisingly, evaporating from them.

And then an oddly cool sensation, unrelated to the wind, passed over her skin. Slocum had only laughed once, hadn't he? He'd never laid a hand on her, for good or for bad. Although she was fairly convinced by her experience that there was no "good" in it.

So, why was she taking it out on him? He'd been kinder to her than anybody else—especially lately. She planted her weight firmly in the saddle, pulled back on the reins, and the horse slowed.

It was a good thing, too. He was lathering, and glad to ease up.

Slocum loped up beside her and signaled for her to rein in a notch. She eased the bay into a trot, then a jog, and Slocum stayed right beside her.

"You ride it out?" he said, as if he knew her thoughts.

She nodded. Slocum wasn't so bad. Slocum was all right, actually.

Well, so far.

She reined in a bit more, until her horse was down to a walk. She said, "Sorry."

"Don't apologize to me, Mrs. Tanglewood," he replied. "Save your sorries for the horses." He wasn't looking at her, but down at her horse's feet. He looked up again. "Doesn't look to have done any damage," he said. "But remember, these horses are unshod. Doesn't help to put more strain on 'em than we have to."

He was lecturing her!

"Nonsense," she said, the old vitriol rising. "Indians—"

"Indians rode unshod ponies, I know," he interrupted, "but they also weren't carryin' heavy saddles and gear and bedrolls."

She narrowed her eyes. "Are you patronizing me, Slocum?"

"Not that I'm aware of, ma'am."

"It certainly sounds to me as if you are," she snapped.

He sighed. "Now, look Mrs. Tanglewood, I'm sorry if I'm doin' something that's tickin' you off. If I am, I sure wish you'd tell me outright, because you're beginnin' to piss me off. I can't see that I'm goin' out of my way to step on your toes. In fact, seems to me that I been doing you nothing but a great big favor ever since I met you."

She said nothing—mainly, because he was right. She felt heat creeping up her neck, and made a point of not looking at him directly.

He had been good to her. He'd probably saved her from the beating of a lifetime, and probably worse. He had no way of knowing just how far Bass could go, but she did. And she was grateful to Slocum for saving her from it.

So why did she have this reaction to him? Why did she always assume the worst?

She was accustomed to it, that was why.

Slocum had held his piece after that little speech, and she finally spoke.

"Excuse me, Slocum," she said in a quiet voice. Her eyes were still trained on the ground ahead. "I'm sorry if I ill-used this horse. I'm sorry I was rude to you. You have, in fact, been very kind to me. It's good of you to take me down to Phoenix."

"Hell, I thought it was damn nice of me not to shoot you for thieving my horse," he said with a tickle of a smile in his voice, and her head automatically turned toward him. He was grinning.

But this time, she actually felt herself grinning back. He was a different sort of fellow, wasn't he? Oh, she could feel the way he looked at her, feel the heat of his gaze traveling over her body, but then, all men looked at her in that way. Perhaps even the nice ones couldn't help it.

And so she decided to overlook this flaw in his nature. Or perhaps, in man's nature.

For now.

"That looks better on you, Mrs. Tanglewood," he added, and it took her a moment to realize that he was talking about the smile on her face.

"Beth," she said, although her voice was still guarded. "Please call me Beth."

The wind had whipped the hell out of her hair, Slocum thought. It was loose and wild and down around her slim shoulders, and he liked it fine, but he didn't mention it. He was going to have to tiptoe pretty carefully with this one, and he knew it.

He thought that maybe he had her pegged now—well, at least as well as any man could peg a woman he'd known for less than twenty-four hours. He figured her whole life had been pretty rotten, and most of it had been at the hands of men—Bass Tanglewood in particular. Maybe she'd learned to just lie down and take it. Most women did, he'd found, no matter how foul the treatment.

Then again, she'd been traveling with the Granger boys. She seemed to be in some sort of command, even though she was technically their prisoner. Was it their fear of her husband?

It was possible, but Slocum didn't think that could account for all of it. And if she'd been "trained" by life to just take whatever it handed out—especially if it came from the hand of man—you would have expected her to act more . . . subservient.

Or something.

Slocum scratched the back of his neck. Maybe he didn't have her figured out too well, after all.

Rome and London Granger were having quite a time of it.

Three times they had started following false leads, although Rome supposed you couldn't exactly call them that.

"Imaginary leads" was more like it.

He felt that they were on the right path now, but damn, it was hard going! Slow, too. Trying to follow a couple of unshod horses over solid rock was like trying to track a catfish in a lake.

There just wasn't that much to go on.

But they'd just come to a promising sign—a small, damp patch on the rock. It looked to have been a bigger spill, just on the verge of evaporating away, and at first he'd thought that probably a bird flying overhead had pissed it out.

Except he'd made London taste it, and it was just plain water.

And the only way he figured that water would appear out here, in the middle of nowhere and nothing, was if somebody had gotten a little sloppy with a canteen.

He figured that could only be one party: Slocum and Mrs. Tanglewood. Christ, didn't she know she was only making it harder on herself? They'd only end up catching her again, but then they'd show up late at the Tanglewood ranch, and Mr. Tanglewood would be fit to be tied.

Rome and London were still surrounded by nothing but rock substrate, and Rome knew they'd been damn lucky to come across the remains of that splash of water.

He looked down at it again. It was nearly gone. He imagined that it would evaporate into invisibility within just a minute or two.

Should they just go on the way they'd been going? Or was Slocum smart enough to have left that sign, just in case they made it this far, and then swing off in a new direction?

"London?" he said.

"What?"

"Here," Rome said, and handed over his spyglass.

London eagerly took it, opened it up, and just before he put it up to his eye, asked, "Where you want I should look?"

"Not yet," Rome said with a shake of his head. "Get up on the horse first."

"Sure, Rome," his brother replied. "Why, I'll be able to see a lot farther from up there."

Rome waited until London was mounted before he said, "Now, stand up."

"On what?"

"On your saddle?"

"Are you crazy?"

"Probably," Rome said, nodding. "I'll grab hold of your feet so's you don't slip."

London stayed just where he was. "You've gone plumb loco, Rome!"

"Gimme that, you idiot," Rome said with a growl, and snatched away the spyglass. "You want somethin' done right, I guess you got to do it yourself."

When London still sat there, staring down at him, Rome hollered, "Get down!" And tried to give off just the right air of disgust.

It worked, because ol' London cringed a bit. But then he set his jaw and said, "No, sir. I'll do it, Rome. Just didn't know you was that serious, was all."

Rome stared at him a moment, then handed the spyglass back up.

After a few minutes of swearing and slipping and sliding and propping up, London finally made it to his knees, and then up to his feet. Rome stood there with a death grip on London's wobbling boots while London held the spyglass to his eye, every muscle in his skinny body tensed.

"Well?" Rome demanded, and London wavered dangerously.

"Don't spook me like that, Rome!" he hollered down. "You want I should break my neck?"

"Can you see anything?" Rome asked, using a little more self-control this time.

London appeared to be scanning the horizon, and then, when he was looking straight to the south, he stopped. "Hold on. Just a second . . ."

Rome ground his teeth. Damn that London! Either he saw something or he didn't.

And at last, London said, "Rome?"

"What!"

"I believe I see somethin' way up there. Looks to be, I don't know . . . maybe a little grove of palo verde or somethin'?"

Excited by London's first words, Rome said, "Get down!"

Slocum and Beth Tanglewood were headed south, due south, toward Phoenix, he was pretty damn sure of it. That little oasis would have to be somewhere that a spring could break through, and that meant it had to be past the rock flow.

If he was right, there'd be plenty of goddamn tracks around it, all right, and a good plain trail afterward!

London fell from the horse for the last few feet, but once he got himself dusted off, Rome deemed him good enough to walk.

Rome slammed the spyglass closed, then shoved it into the saddlebag. "You all right?" he asked London, mostly just to be polite since he'd already decided. He grabbed hold of the saddle's horn and stepped up into the seat.

"I suppose," said London, rubbing at his hip. "Why do I always gotta be the one to walk? It's your horse they made off with!"

"You won't be walkin' this time, London," said Rome, and set off at a slow jog.

"Hey!" shouted London, but kept up a limping trot beside him.

8

Joe and Harley had just come on the place where Slocum had pulled his horse's shoes, and they stopped there to water their own mounts from the canteens. And have themselves a little think on what they saw in the tracks.

Joe could just see the traces of one shod mount moving on to the south. He supposed he was one of the few living trackers that could make any sense of a sign that faint. He was that good, all right.

Except for these two fellows ahead of him. They were tracking Slocum, too. He had to admit, they were better than he ever hoped to be. That is, if they were on the right trail.

Of course, they might be following nothing. They might have been duped by some trick of light on stone—or maybe they'd just plain given up.

But somehow, he didn't think so.

Who were these boys, anyway? He felt a grudging admiration for them, even though they were going to end up dead if they had any bright ideas about getting Slocum's cash for themselves.

"Now what?" asked Harley. He leaned against his saddle, lazily rolling a smoke.

"I reckon we ought to turn south," Joe answered. He patted his gray on the shoulder, then put away his damp nosebag. "After those other boys."

Harley shook out his match and tossed it down. "You
that sure they've got a line on Slocum's trail?"

Maybe you're not as dumb as you act, buddy, Joe
thought. *You seen those tracks to the south as sure as I did.*

But he said, "Nope, I ain't certain, but it's the best
chance we got. And it's the one I'm gonna take."

Harley nodded. "Fair 'nough," he said thoughtfully, before he blew out a plume of smoke.

"Hope you realize we just left one helluva trail back there,"
Slocum said as they continued on south. "Hope it made
you feel better."

And that was the truth. It sure hadn't done him any
good, though.

She was silent for a moment, then said, "It did. But why
does it matter? I thought we lost them for good when you
pulled the shoes off the horses."

"Said maybe," Slocum replied. "No tellin'. I'm thinking
that maybe we ought to swing over to Cholla and see a
blacksmith before we go any farther."

"Why?"

"Because that gelding of yours is lookin' a little gimpy
in the rear."

She frowned at him. "It doesn't feel like he's limping."

Slocum sighed. "Well, he will be before long."

He reined Panther in to the side of her horse, forcing it
to the east. Beth scowled at him, but didn't fight. She went
along with it without further comment.

He sure wished she'd be more consistently . . . well,
pleasant. Sure, she had an awfully pretty scowl, but she had
a radiant smile. At least, what he'd seen of it so far.

"We might have to trade that bay of yours in on a sound

horse if he goes lame before we get to town," he said. "Would that get you ruffled?"

She shrugged. "The gelding's not mine. It's Rome's."

"Fine."

"Slocum?"

"What?"

"I'm sorry."

He arched a brow. There were any number of possibilities—and good reasons—for her apology. "Sorry about what?"

"Sorry that I've been kind of . . . uneven with you. You must think I'm half-crazy. I wouldn't blame you if you did."

He thumbed back his hat. "Well, you have been kind of up and down on me," he said, then lied, "I thought it was somethin' I was doing."

"No, not at all," she said. "I'm just . . . confused, you know? Guess I'm taking it out on you. I'm grateful that you saved me, but then you said we were going to Paris, and I had my mind all set on it, you know?"

She paused, then went on, "Sort of like when a man's about to die of thirst and all of a sudden he gets offered a whole, clear mountain lake."

"And then finds out it was only a damp stain on the ground?" Slocum asked.

"That's about the size of it," she said. "I should have known right from the start you were only trying to pull the wool over the Grangers' eyes. I was plain stupid."

"No, you weren't," Slocum said, even though he secretly agreed with her.

"Yes," she said firmly, "I was."

Slocum chuckled. "Have it your way. In any case, apology accepted. Now, no need to get grumpy all over again, Beth," he added when that scowl started to wad up her features once more. "I just can't seem to win with you. I agree with you and you think I'm . . ."

"Patronizing?" she offered.

"Yeah, that," he answered. "And if I disagree, I'm trying to push you around. The truth be told, Beth, I'm just tryin' to get to Phoenix—and get you there, too—in one piece."

"I know," she said, so softly that he barely heard her. And then, quite suddenly, she seemed to turn on him. "Just what do you mean by 'in one piece'?"

"Huh?"

"What do you plan on doing to me on the way there, Slocum?" she demanded angrily. "Are you calling me a 'piece'? Just who in the hell do you think you are, anyway?"

"Nothing, Beth, nobody! Christ! You're crazy."

"I'll show you crazy!" she shouted, and raised her arm to quirt her poor bay into another gallop.

But Slocum's arm was faster than hers. Before her whip landed, he reached out and took a tight grip on her reins. When her quirt landed on the bay's rump, the bay swung wildly and skittered out, but only its backside. Its head stayed put, tethered to Slocum's hand, and Beth glared at him.

"You try to run this horse again, and I *will* give you something to holler about," Slocum said through gritted teeth.

"I knew it," she shouted. "You're all alike. Each and every one of you!"

"I said it before and I'll say it again, honey," he growled. "You're plumb crazy. Now, I'm gonna lead you on into Cholla. We're gonna go straight to the blacksmith's and see about these horses. And then you can do whatever the hell you want."

Slocum was as irritated as a boil just coming to a head, but he didn't let the full extent of it show. He simply hung on to her reins and began leading her horse toward Cholla. If she wanted to start walking and hopped off, headed in the opposite direction, that was her business. He had just about played out his string.

She was a bleeding lunatic, that was for sure. Oh, she'd had a hard time of it, that was for certain. But there weren't enough mitigating circumstances in the whole county for Slocum to put up with this crud any longer than he had to.

Having left the little oasis behind them, the expert trackers, Rome and London Granger, had little trouble following Slocum and Beth's tracks. They walked while Slocum and Beth had galloped, of course, for London was still on foot. It was slow, but both men were positive that this was the right trail.

"Can I ride now?" London whined pitifully. "I swan, Rome, my leg and hip are gettin' sorer by the minute! If I don't get off my leg, I'm gonna be lame for life! I swear it!"

Rome looked over at him, and decided to have a little mercy for his griping brother. He swung down from the saddle.

"All right," he said. "I reckon you can take a turn now."

As London happily mounted the horse, Rome added, "But don't get too comfortable up there."

"All right, Rome," London answered happily and clucked to the horse. "Fair enough."

But Rome had stopped, and was bending low to the ground. "Hold up, there, London."

London reined in the gelding and leaned backward in the saddle. "What you got there, Rome?

Rome stared down at an infinitesimal break in the track, no larger than a human hair. But it was repeated, in the last track and this—same horse, same hoof. Without saying anything, he rose and walked ahead to where the next stride would have taken that hoof.

And there it was again.

"Reckon they don't know it," he said, standing up and dusting his hands, "but those two have got trouble coming."

"What kind?" asked London. "I couldn't see nothin' from up here."

And you sure didn't climb down to have a closer look, did you, brother? Rome thought.

But he said, "One of those horses is growing a little ol' crack in his hoof that's going to turn itself into a big ol' split. Probably my horse, too, goddamn it."

"It's goin' lame?" asked London, suddenly all smiles.

"Sooner or later," Rome said. He started forward at a fast, renewed walk, his spurs jingling as he went. London clucked to the horse to keep up.

"That Slocum's no fool," Rome said as he marched. "He'll see it. Hell, the sonofabitch'll probably sense it! And he'll want to get to the closest blacksmith. I've heard he's practically crazed when it comes to horses."

"I heard that, too," London mused. "Phoenix, you reckon?"

Rome shook his head. "No, Cholla."

Harley had fallen asleep on his horse, Joe French noted.

It wasn't an unusual feat for men who spent of lot of time on horseback. Harley's chestnut just kept right up with Joe's gray, slowly rocking Harley back and forth in the saddle.

Now, this little occurrence wouldn't have been bad or good or even worthy of remark, except that sometimes, Harley talked in his sleep.

And today, he was babbling like a lunatic.

"Ten thousand," Joe had heard him say at least a dozen times.

Usually, at night, he couldn't make out a word that Harley said, but today, for some reason, he was spewing out crystal-clear sentences. Maybe it had something to do with his upright position. Maybe it was because it was afternoon, not night.

Joe didn't know about that. He only knew that he was mad, because Joe was sounding awfully proprietary about the whole of that ten thousand Slocum was carrying.

Joe didn't like that at all.

In fact, Joe was pissed off in the worst possible way.

"Mine, all mine," mumbled Harley. "Gonna have a ranch. Gonna have horses. Cattle. Set out the corn, Mabel. Save me some'a them peas for the roof."

"Mabel?" Joe muttered. Who the hell was Mabel? And why the hell would anybody want peas up on a roof?

Well, it was Harley's dream, he supposed.

"Ten thousand," Harley mumbled again, his eyes closed, his head lolling, and a big, stupid smile covering his sleeping face. "Shoot that dumb Joe dead as a stump. I'll have the red ones, Ma."

"That's enough," Joe said, loud enough that it woke poor Harley from his slumber.

And just as Harley turned sleepily toward Joe to see what was going on, Joe shot him through the neck.

Blood spurted bright, and Joe ducked to avoid being splattered by it.

Harley only lived long enough to get out half a strangled scream. He fell off his horse, dead before he hit the ground, and Joe holstered his gun.

He rode on a few feet farther, then dismounted and stripped the tack off Harley's horse, setting the chestnut free on the open plain. With a little canteen water and a rag, he took a few cursory wipes at the few drops of Harley's blood that had stained his cuff.

He left Harley's tack in a pile not far from the body and the pool of blood it lay in, took the saddlebags for himself, and mounted his gray again.

"Greedy trash," he said as he looked down at Harley for the last time. It had been nice of Harley to let him in on this Slocum thing, but Harley had forgotten one important thing: When you told Joe French it was an even split, it had best be just that.

"Never liked that sonofabitch, anyhow," he muttered.

He rode off, going on down to the little oasis, which had just come into view, and as he neared it, he began to whistle.

9

By the time Slocum and Beth made it to Cholla, they were both on foot. Beth's mount had started to limp visibly, and Slocum could see that the hoof was starting to split. Since he didn't think it would do Panther any good to bear the weight of two riders, he'd walked the rest of the way into town with Beth.

She was getting crazier by the moment, if he was any judge, and he didn't think it was an act. At one point, she'd sung "Three Cheers for Billy" at the top of her voice (and Slocum had to admit it was a nice one) then laughed and talked about getting away from Bass Tanglewood for once and for all.

And roughly two minutes later, she was berating Slocum for, well, he wasn't quite sure what it was he'd done to set her off, but it must have been something powerfully bad.

Anyhow, to hear her tell it.

He was damned glad when the town finally came into sight.

But he wasn't so glad, once he got a little closer.

Cholla had never been much more than a wide spot in the road, but these days it wasn't even that. It seemed that Slocum had last seen Cholla in its heyday, for now tumbleweeds sat unmolested, waiting for a breeze on Main Street. The livery, the saloon, and the mercantile were deserted.

In fact, the town was totally and completely without population.

"Now what?" Beth demanded.

She appeared tired and dirty. A thick layer of dust rose a good foot up her skirts. And she didn't look like she was in one of her rare and fleeting good moods.

Slocum tried the pump at the old horse trough in front of the saloon. Fortunately, some thoughtful soul had left a glass canning jar, full of water, tied to the handle with a string, so he had no trouble priming it. After a few dry pumps of the handle, it spewed out brown water, then clear.

"There," he said. "You keep workin' that pump till you get yourself enough water, and then you get cleaned up. I'm goin' back to the livery to see if somebody left his far-rier tools around."

Both her eyebrows hiked up. "Get cleaned up? You expect me to take a bath? Out here?"

"No, I expect you to do whatever you want. But I ain't haulin' no water for you."

She stomped her foot and folded her arms, but she spat, "Fine!" She turned her back on him with a certain degree of finality.

Shrugging, Slocum wandered back down to the livery. Before he went inside, to the horses, he glanced back up the street. There was Beth, working away on that pumping like a madwoman.

But then, she was half loco, wasn't she?

He shook his head, then went inside.

By the time he finished at the stable, it was nearly dark. He'd been able to scare up enough materials to shoe both horses, but the heat from the forge had about done him in.

Once again, he was awfully glad that he hadn't taken up the farrier's trade.

There was hay left in the barn, although not much, but it wasn't mildewed. He fed that and some of the oats he'd brought along to the horses.

"Sorry, Panther," he said as he patted the gelding's neck. "Sorry it ain't better chuck. But once we get to Phoenix, you'll eat like a king."

Panther gave no sign of caring one way or the other, and ground his oats happily.

Slocum had carried buckets of water—both for the shoeing and for the horses's stalls—from the pump in front of the barn. And then, when everything else was done, he refilled the priming jar, then undressed and lowered himself into the trough. Crazy Beth was nowhere to be seen.

After he got himself good and plain-water washed, he dressed again, then scooped up more water in a bucket for a shave. No use fouling the horses' drinking water with soap. He shaved himself by the last rays of the sun in the pocket mirror he carried with him.

At least Beth had had sense enough not to toss it on the ground, along with practically everything else he owned.

And then, girding his loins and dreading the worst, he grabbed the saddlebags and struck off for the saloon. He knew they had rooms upstairs since it had served Cholla as both the hotel and whorehouse, once upon a time, and Beth had probably headed inside.

He'd see if she was in a good enough mood to scrape together some dinner for them.

When he pushed through the bat-wing doors of the saloon, however, he got a surprise. Where he had expected cobwebs and dust, as well as vermin, he found a spanking clean saloon. Everything was swept and dusted, the glasses polished, the windows washed, and he smelled the odor— and a good one, at that—of food cooking.

He stood there for a moment, dumbfounded, and finally called, "Beth?"

"Supper will be ready in a minute, Andy," she called cheerily from the kitchen, back behind the bar. "Just make yourself comfy, and it'll be right out! There's whiskey on the bar, if you're so inclined."

Slocum took off his hat and ran his fingers through his hair before he rubbed hard at his forehead. Who the hell was Andy?

Jesus! What was it with this gal?

"I went to the mercantile," she continued happily from behind the closed door. "There wasn't much there, but I found enough to make us a good meal. Dried apples and flour and sugar and lard, and tinned meat and vegetables and such."

Slocum found the whiskey—a half bottle—and poured himself a shot, which he threw back in one gulp.

"Do you like lima beans?" her disembodied voice continued cheerily. "I do, but some folks don't. I made pintos and peas in case you don't. Could you get the door for me?"

Slocum made his feet move toward the door and pushed it inward. There stood Beth, a white apron neatly tied over her dress, with a bowl of beans in one hand, a plate of biscuits in the other, and a big grin on her face.

"Let me help you with that," he said as he kicked the doorstop into place with the toe of his boot.

She noted the movement and exclaimed, "Oh, how clever of you!"

Slocum just stared at her.

She handed him the beans and biscuits, then daintily turned and picked up two more bowls. The kitchen was as clean as the bar room, Slocum noted. He didn't comment, though. He wanted to enjoy his meal with no unpleasantness, and the lord knew she could go off at the drop of a hat.

They ate a lingering meal by the light of a kerosene lamp, and he had to admit that she was a pretty fair cook.

Considering what she had to work with, that was. He didn't talk during dinner. She did, though. A lot. He just nodded.

Most of what she had to say was just lunatic fancies, like how they were going to have to get the barn finished before winter. She called him Andy half the time, and he didn't correct her. He didn't want to start anything.

She was getting worse, and Slocum was well aware of it. But she had some lucid times, when she knew where she was, and what Slocum had saved her from. And she was grateful.

In fact, they got halfway through dessert—a good, dried-apple pie—before she turned nasty on him.

"I supposed you want me to take your whippin' now," she suddenly snarled.

Slocum blinked. He hadn't said or done a thing to get her going. But finally, he said, "No ma'am, I sure don't."

"If you expect me to furnish the handcuffs, you're sorely mistaken."

Slocum pushed back his chair. "Look, lady . . ."

"Don't 'look, lady' me! I know your kind! You take a lady out for dinner and then you expect the world in return!"

She stood abruptly, tipping the table over sideways in her haste. Slocum watched his slice of pie sail across the room.

"Stop it!" he shouted, hoping to jar her back to reality.

But it didn't work. She just shouted, "I will not!" right back in his face, then picked up a bowl from the floor and threw it at him.

He ducked just in time, and it crashed into the wall behind him and shattered.

He figured that the best place to be, right at the moment, was anyplace but here. He grabbed his hat off the chair he'd thrown it on and turned toward the doors.

And then stopped.

London and Rome Granger stood in the doorway. They were smiling smugly, and both had their guns drawn.

They were pointed squarely at him.

10

"My goodness," Rome said, and he made the word *my* last a long time. "Lookee here, London. The great and mighty Slocum, runnin' from a woman."

"Beats everything, don't it, Rome?" London drawled, a grin spreading over his face. He turned toward a spittoon, aimed, and hit it.

"Pigs!" Beth shouted, and hurled a platter at them. Both Granger brothers ducked to the side as it smashed against the door's frame. "What? All three of you, now? You want me to pleasure all three of you, you sonsofbitches?"

Slocum took the opportunity to jump over the bar. He crouched behind it, his Colt drawn and ready. But it didn't look as if he would get a chance to use it for a while, because Beth was going on a real tear.

Plates crashed, glassware shattered.

"Missus?" London's voice carried in from the street. Apparently, he'd retreated to the street. "Mrs. Tanglewood?"

Slocum crawled to the far end of the bar.

"Ain't gonna hurt you, Mrs. Tanglewood," Rome called. He was outside again, too. "We just wanna—"

"Men!" Beth shouted, and Slocum heard something else

break violently. "You go straight to hell, Andy, and take your drunken friends with you!"

"But ma'am—" Rome tried again.

This time she must have thrown the crockery straight through the door because London let out a loud whoop, then a curse word.

And then Rome hissed, "Get out of the line of fire, you fool!"

"I hate you!" Beth railed. "I hate you all!"

It seemed that everybody had forgotten all about him for the moment, and Slocum slipped through the door and into the kitchen without attracting Beth's attention. She was too busy shouting and picking up broken crockery—for there weren't any whole pieces left—and hurling the biggest pieces against the wall or out the door.

Slocum moved quietly through the kitchen while Rome and London Granger argued and pleaded with her from out front. He paused, however, by the table. She'd left the pie out, and he cut himself a big slice in a hurry. The way things were going, there was no telling when he'd get homemade apple pie again.

Pie in his left hand, his gun in his right, he soundlessly slipped out the back door and into the darkened alley. And as he worked his way along the back of the building, he ate.

It was damn good pie.

And these were damn strange circumstances.

He figured that, regardless of what plans they had for him, old Rome and London wouldn't do anything to hurt Beth Tanglewood. They seemed to be going out of their way to kid-glove her back home, to her husband.

Slocum knew who Bass Tanglewood was, all right.

He couldn't say he'd want to go back to him, either, if he were in Beth's shoes. Bass Tanglewood was rich, richer than Croesus. He'd made his money mining gold during the rush, then parlayed it into an even vaster fortune. Railroads, beef, shipping, timber: you name it and Bass Tangle-wood had his hand in it somewhere.

Slocum only knew Tanglewood through rumors and newspaper articles. The rumors were juicier, mainly because Tanglewood owned most of the newspapers farther west. But they all fit with what Beth had told him, when she was in her right mind. Or minds. Bass Tanglewood had been sick, all right, sick and dying in New Orleans, and then had made a miraculous recovery.

The last he'd heard, Bass Tanglewood had bought some giant old rancho—stole it, more likely—in southern California, just outside Los Angeles, and retired in style. Although he supposed a man like Tanglewood never really retired.

He hadn't heard that old Tanglewood had a lunatic wife, though.

Or that he was so fond of roughing up women.

Mainly, he'd heard that Bass Tanglewood was a bastard—both literally and figuratively.

So far, Bass's hirelings and wife hadn't done anything to change his initial appraisal of the man.

He gulped the last bite of pie, then eased toward the edge of the building closest to the street. There was still a lot of shouting going on, but not so much breakage. She was running out of things—and pieces of things—to hurl at the Grangers.

Rome and London were still trying to sweet-talk her out the front door, though. He figured they probably had more experience with her than he had. They must figure that sooner or later, she'd do one of those mental turnarounds and be easier to handle.

'Course, if it had been him, he just would have gone down to the livery to sleep, and waited her out.

The hell he would!

He'd have thrown his hands in the air and gone to Phoenix, that's what!

"Shit," he muttered under his breath.

He supposed he could do just that—sneak down to the livery and saddle up Panther and just take off to the south. It'd serve all three of these jackasses right.

But he knew it would plague him, not knowing what had happened to Beth. No matter what, she didn't deserve to go back to Bass Tanglewood.

Besides, those two out front of the saloon had bashed him over the head and made off with his horse. There was still a score to settle.

Silently, he blew air out through pursed lips, took careful aim at Rome, who was closest to the light coming through the saloon window, and fired.

Instantaneously, Rome's gun went flying, Rome screamed and shoved his fingers in his mouth, and London fired wild, missing Slocum by a mile.

Before the Grangers could scramble into the shadows, Slocum called, "Stay right where you are, or the next slug does more than hit your gun!"

"Damn you!" cried Rome around the gag of his hand. He hadn't moved an inch.

"Drop it, London," Slocum shouted.

Reluctantly, London eased his grip on his pistol, and it fell to the ground with a soft *plop* and a small cloud of dust.

"Well?" Beth was shouting from inside, asking a question he hadn't heard. "Well?" she repeated.

"Beth!" he hollered as he stepped out from behind the building's corner. "Beth! You all right?"

Not that he expected a civil answer.

And he didn't get one. In fact, he didn't get any answer at all.

"Stop pushin'!" London hollered at him as Slocum moved the Granger brothers through the bat-wing saloon doors at gunpoint.

"I ain't pushin' you," Rome growled. "Just shut up and keep movin'."

To tell the truth, Rome was pretty much amazed that he was still alive, considering that he'd been shot—or rather, that he'd had a gun shot out of his hand—and considering who'd done the shooting. His hand was beginning to swell a little, but he could still move his fingers and had already decided it wasn't broken. It was just sprained enough to feel like it.

He couldn't figure out why Slocum had chosen to bounce a slug off his handgun instead of filling his skull with lead. If things had been the other way round, if Rome had been some big-deal gunslinger on the wrong end of a stolen horse, he would have gunned him down in a split second.

"Sit down, the both of you," Slocum said from behind him.

Rome picked up a chair, righted it, and sat down. London aped him. Mrs. Tanglewood was over by the bar, quiet for once, and just watching them curiously.

"This is all your fault," he growled at her, and London echoed his sentiment. Frankly, at the moment Rome didn't much care what Bass Tanglewood would think.

But Crazy Beth looked at them, then giggled.

"Quiet," Slocum barked. At both of them, and Beth. And they all shut up.

In fact, Mrs. Tanglewood started to quietly cry.

Slocum snapped, "Beth!" and sniffling, she cringed.

"W-what?"

Slocum closed his eyes for a second—like maybe he was willing himself not to slap her, Rome thought, and he sure couldn't hold that against him—and then said, more calmly, "Beth, could you please find me some rope, or maybe some old drape sashes from upstairs?"

She looked at him like he'd just asked for an elephant. But he repeated the request, and then she seemed to understand. She went upstairs, supposedly to look.

Slocum picked up another chair from the floor, flipped it around, and sat down opposite Rome. He slung his arms over the back of it, but still held the gun on him. He wiggled it a little, and Rome sat up a little straighter.

"I'm impressed," Slocum said.

"Huh?" London said. "What for?"

Rome ignored his brother. He nodded at Slocum, and said, "Thanks. Considering the source, it's a right compliment. You gonna kill us now?"

Next to him, he felt London jerk abruptly.

But Slocum just sat there, like he was thinking it over.

The bastard.

And then finally he said, "Not right away. Got some questions first. Like, how'd you trail us over that rock?"

Rome felt his chest puff out a little, but quickly reminded himself that he was in a bad sort of a situation, here, and said, "A metal splinter."

Slocum shook his head. "Damn. Thought I got 'em all."

London had relaxed a tad, and he said, "Then later, we got sorta lost, but we found where you'd spilled some water. There was just a tad of it left, but Rome said taste it and I did, and it was water, all right, and—"

"Shut up, London," Rome said.

But London went on, "Rome made me stand up on my saddle and I seen the spring—seen the trees around it, anyhow—and I says, 'Rome, I think I see some trees way up there, to the south,' and he says, 'That's where they're headed, then,' and I says—"

"Quiet!" Slocum and Rome thundered, as one.

Upstairs, Beth was busy pulling down dusty drapery sashes, although she hardly knew why. Slocum had asked for them, hadn't he?

She didn't remember.

Again.

She felt full, so she must have eaten, and it was dark outside, really dark. And she had this nagging, itchy feeling that Rome and London were close by.

But they couldn't be, could they?

What time was it?

It was obvious that she'd lost some time. "Gone missing," is what she had called it for some time. Well, privately, anyhow. Beth has "gone missing" for a little while.

She gathered up the sashes—whether she had enough or not was anybody's guess—and started back down the stairs with them. Voices carried up to her.

Slocum.

And Rome and London.

She closed her eyes for a moment, telling herself not to panic, and took a surreptitious look around the bend of the landing.

They were there, all right, but Slocum was holding a gun on them. Beth let out an audible sigh, at which Slocum turned to look up at her. She stepped forward.

"Good girl," he said. "You got them. Are they rotted or are they still strong enough?"

Quickly, her mind turned over and began to spin. She said, "They're all right, I believe," and started the rest of the way down. Slocum had trapped the Grangers, who, by some miracle, must have tracked them. She guessed that Slocum had sent her to get something to tie them up. This was all good.

But it wasn't good if that little gallop she'd taken earlier today was responsible for their presence.

That much, she was sure of, and so she handed over the drape sashes rather sheepishly. And then she looked around her.

"What happened in here?" she asked. What had happened to the dusty, deserted saloon? It looked to have been dusted and scrubbed, and then purposely recoated with spattered food and broken crockery!

Who on earth had done this?

And then, without saying a word, she knew. She knew from prior experience, she knew from all her instincts, and she knew by the looks on Rome's and London's faces that she'd done it.

In a small voice, she said, "I'll start cleaning up, shall I, Slocum?"

"I'll help just as soon as I get these two roped in," he replied without looking at her.

My goodness. She'd never noticed how handsome he was! How could she have missed that?

"All right, sugar," she said, and when Slocum's head whipped around, a look of pure puzzlement spreading over his face, she simply winked at him.

11

It was almost too dark to travel, but Joe kept on. He was on foot, walking his horse and keeping a close eye on the tracks before him. It had been an easy trail to follow ever since he left the oasis.

Slocum was headed somewhere specific, that was certain. One of his horses had a bad hoof, and he was making a beeline for someplace to patch it up, Joe figured.

To tell the truth, he was pretty impressed with those boys who were trailing him, and who were making an even easier trail for him to follow.

The night suddenly darkened, and he looked up. Damn clouds, covering the moon again. A fellow would think that a place with so many clouds might have some rain now and then, but no such luck. Maybe they were going over to New Mexico to let loose their water.

Sighing, he stopped in his tracks.

He was tired, and his gray was tired, even though he'd been walking it for the last half-hour. "All right, Nickel," he said to the horse, and rested his hand on its neck. "Let's have a breather. Hell, let's have the rest of the night. Even if it lightened up some, my eyes are too bleary to track anymore, anyhow."

As he began to unfasten the horse's girth, he muttered, "We'll catch him tomorrow. Mayhap those boys that are trackin' him have caught him already. Hell, maybe they've all three killed each other!"

He slid the saddle off and set it on the ground, then draped his saddle blanket over it.

"I kinda like that idea, Nickel." He pulled a pair of hobbles from his saddlebags, snugged them on the horse's front legs, then exchanged bridle for halter.

"Figure that's the best way," he said. He poured feed into a nosebag and strapped it on the horse's head. To the sound of molars grinding oats, he bit off a new plug of tobacco, then stumbled around in the dark, picking up chunks of dead brush and a few sticks.

"Yessir, be awful nice to just find 'em up there, all dead, and with that cash just for the pluckin' up," he said around his chaw. "Easy money. Then it's up to San Francisco for me, and off to the horse dealer's for you." He tipped his head, reconsidering. "Or maybe the glue factory. You ain't gettin' any younger, you know."

And then he laughed.

It was a purely evil sound.

This time, Slocum hadn't gagged Rome and London, although, once he'd gotten them tied up, he went down to the stable, leading their one horse behind him, and brought back the only chunk of rope left in the barn. The last piece that wasn't in use, that was.

When he came back up the street, following the glow from the bar's door and windows like they were beacons instead of faint orange glows, he paused a moment before going inside. He couldn't see Beth anywhere, but he could hear the Grangers talking.

"How much more time you figure we got, Rome?" London said.

"Before he kills us like a couple of stoats at slaughter, or before I kill you for bothering me with fool questions?"

"I mean, before he does . . . whatever he's gonna do with us." London paused. "You really think he's gonna kill us?"

Rome said, "London, how dumb can you be? We stole his horse. We tried to make off with Mrs. Tanglewood. Again. What do you think?"

London let out a sigh. "He's gonna kill us, ain't he?"

"Wouldn't you, London, if you was in his boots?"

London didn't have an answer for that.

Outside the door, slouched against the building, Slocum smiled, then straightened. He didn't think these boys were killers. In fact, he suspected they weren't much more than gold-star trackers. Of course, that was a talent unto itself, but it didn't make them toughs, just good at paying attention.

They did work for Bass Tanglewood, though.

He had to keep remembering that part.

He walked into the bar and dropped the coil of rope on a table, which had been righted during his absence. "Beth do this?" he asked when he saw that somebody had been cleaning up a little, too.

"Wasn't us," said London, dully. He looked at his boots. Rome just sat there.

"I'm not gonna kill you," Slocum said, to put them both out of their misery.

Rome looked up and London sagged against his drape-sash bonds. London whispered, "Thank you, Lord, thank you!"

Slocum went on, " 'Course, I'd be justified. You boys stole my horse." His hand went to his head, which still had quite a goose egg on it. "Near about killed me, too. But I decided I ain't gonna hold a grudge. This time, anyhow."

Rome nodded, then said, "I take it there's gonna be a deal in here, someplace?"

Slocum said, "There is," before he headed toward the kitchen.

"She ain't there," London called, before Slocum made it to the door. He nodded toward the staircase. "She's upstairs. You gonna untie us?"

"Not yet," Slocum replied. He started toward the stairs, then, on second thought, he went back to where the Grangers were tied. Taking the rope off the table, he grabbed one end, let the coil drop to the floor, and tied the Grangers a second time.

"For a man who bears us no malice, you appear to be takin' a few too many cautions," Rome said at one point, and he sounded leery.

Slocum replied, "Sorry, Rome, but I don't trust you. That's one thing we need to get straight right up front. You understand?"

Rome nodded. "Reckon I do."

"Well, I don't!" London said in a voice entirely too whiney.

"Shut up," said Rome.

"There," Slocum muttered as he gave the knot a last tug. "That oughta hold you a while. You boys were plenty damn quick skinning out of those ropes this morning. Figure I needed to give it a little extra care this time."

London, who seemed to take this as a compliment, suddenly beamed and said, "Thanks. We practice all the time, me and Rome."

Rome growled, "Shut up," again.

Slocum didn't smile until he'd turned his back on them and headed toward the stairs.

He found her in the third room he checked.

She was waiting in the bed, and she was already naked. When she sat up and smiled at him, she let the covers slip to her waist.

Slocum was instantly hard, although if anybody had

asked him three minutes before, he would have said it was impossible to get that stiff, that fast. But he didn't step into the room.

She moved the covers on the closest side of the bed back, making a space for him.

"Well, cowboy?" she purred. "What's taking you so long?"

Cowboy?

"The name's Slocum, not cowboy," he said softly.

She had high breasts, high and probably firm, and her waist was tiny, her skin flawless. He swallowed, hard. She was crazy, too. This wasn't her. He wasn't sure who she was this time, but she wasn't herself.

"All right, Slocum," she said, slowly batting her lashes at him. "What's the matter? You shy? From that bulge in the front of your britches, you don't appear the shy type."

She grinned at him.

He figured that he'd probably kick himself later, but he willed himself down.

"This isn't you, Beth," he said.

"Oh?" she replied as she peeled back the rest of the covers. Languidly, she swung her legs over the bedside. "Then just who might I be, cowboy?" she asked, still grinning seductively.

"Stop it, Beth," he said, and his voice came out broken. Damn her, anyway!

Now she was slowly crossing the room toward him, a beckon in her eyes, in her hands, in her full, ripe mouth, and he was erect again. Her long slim legs led up to gently belled hips . . .

He took a step backward. This whole thing was a real bad idea. He just had to convince *her* of that.

But she was in his arms before he knew what hit him. He was just bending to taste her lips when his eyes fell on her shoulder, onto a patch of skin that hadn't been exposed before.

He pulled back.

She stood there, blinking. "Darlin'? What's the trouble?"

He put his hands on her shoulders and turned her around.

"Oh, my dear Lord, Beth . . ." he breathed.

Women always told him he was a maze of scars, but he had nothing on her. Scar tissue crisscrossed her back and buttocks, and the tops of her thighs. Burn marks, old and new, were scattered across her skin. A jagged line of welted tissue cut a hard, thick line straight across her buttocks.

"Bass Tanglewood did this to you?" he asked softly.

All of a sudden, she stiffened.

She whirled around, saw him, and tried to cover herself with her hands while she backed away from him, toward the shelter of the covers.

"What . . . what are you doing in here?" she cried, flustered and embarrassed. She finally backed her way to the bed and wrapped the linens around her faster than a frog on a stove lid.

It would have been funny, Slocum thought, if he were seeing it in a play, but it sure wasn't funny in real life.

"Beth, what'd he do to you?" he asked.

"What were you planning to do to me?" she screeched, and her hand went to an old figurine on the nightstand. She picked it up and threatened him with it. "How did you get in my room? I'll call the manager!"

She raised the hand with the figurine, and cried, "Help! Someone, help!"

And then she threw it at him.

It smashed against the wall beside him.

He flinched, but stood his ground. "Beth," he said, "just calm down. I ain't goin' to—"

She reached for something else to throw, but couldn't find anything. Hopping backward and up on the bed, she retreated to its farthest corner, pulling the sheets up to her chin.

She was terrified, Slocum realized. In fact, she was shivering with fear.

He backed out of the room and closed the door between them and just stood there a moment, shaking his head. What the hell was wrong with her, anyhow? There must be a whole nest of people living inside her head!

He'd never seen anything like it, and he hoped never to again. At least he didn't have an erection anymore. And then he idly wondered why this was a *good* thing.

Hell, his whole world was going as topsy-turvy as hers was!

He gave a final shake to his head and walked back down the hall, back down the stairs, and back to his immediate problem: What to do with Rome and London?

12

"You boys eat yet?" was the question Slocum had asked when he got back downstairs.

Rome and London had no need to answer. London's loud stomach growl told Slocum the answer.

So he unbound Rome, then held his gun on him while he freed his brother, and they proceeded into the kitchen. He sat at the table, munching another piece of apple pie, while they cut a swath through the pots and pans, gobbling up the last of what Beth had cooked.

All in all, he imagined they got a pretty good feed out of it, and likely the best they'd had in a long spell.

"Mrs. Tanglewood do the cookin'?" London asked as he pulled out a chair, eyed Slocum's Colt once again, then out himself a slab of apple pie.

"Yup," Slocum answered, his brow cocked, and waited. It was the first complete sentence either brother had uttered since they entered the kitchen.

He didn't have long to wait.

"One time, when we was bringin' her back?" London continued around a mouthful of pie. "She got in the right mood and made us a whole wild turkey supper, didn't she, Rome? Outta the stuff in our saddlebags and the game we shot!"

London closed his eyes and rubbed his stomach. "My goodness sakes, that was quite a meal!"

Rome, who had seated himself while London was speaking, cut himself a piece of pie and nodded.

They both looked quite a bit tamer at the moment than when he'd first met them, Slocum thought. He considered putting his gun away, but didn't. It was still too early in the game, and trust didn't come easily to him. Especially, trust for a couple of horse thieves.

Rome took a big bite of the pie he held in his hand, and added, "She's a real piece of work, all right. As lunatic as they come." He looked from his pie to Slocum. "We heard you up there," he said. "The loud parts, anyhow."

Slocum said, "Loud was the most of it, all right."

"I'd like to say that I'm right sorry about thievin' your horse, Slocum," London said. He looked sincere enough.

Slocum didn't answer him.

Rome added a reluctant, "Yeah." And then he added, "It was just that we was short a mount and in a hurry, and you happened along . . ."

Slocum grumbled, "Lucky me."

"We didn't know who you was, right off," London said, in a whiney, simpering voice that interfered, somewhat, with his chewing. "If we had, we would'a made sure you was good and dead before we—"

"Don't help, London," Rome snapped.

And Slocum grinned.

Everything was quiet upstairs, which was a great relief to Slocum. The last thing he needed, right at the moment, was one of Beth's fits. He didn't know what else to call them.

He wondered if he'd even met the real, true Beth, yet.

If there was one.

After the lengthy process of taking the Grangers to the outhouse and letting them use it, one at a time, then tying them up once more, he finally sat down at one of the tables in the saloon, and heaved a sigh. He wished he had about four hands, and he wasn't quite sure what to do next.

He supposed that he could just ride out in the morning, and leave them all to do whatever they wanted.

Or he could take Beth, and leave the Grangers behind to struggle out of their bonds by their own steam.

Or he could take along all three of them.

He honestly didn't know.

And he also didn't know what the hell he'd do with them once he got to Phoenix.

It was a dilemma.

Rome broke the silence. "So, what you gonna do with us, Slocum?"

Slocum just looked at him for a long time, then asked, "What do you think I should do with the two of you?" He was honestly curious.

He knew what London thought, because his only answer was to hang his head. But Rome seemed to actually consider it.

"I know what I'd do, if I was you," he said. For not the first time, Slocum wondered where he'd gotten that scar. It was a bad one.

"What's that?"

"Well," Rome drawled, "I reckon I'd ask us how well we liked workin' for Bass Tanglewood. And our answer would probably be, 'Not so much.' "

Slocum figured he knew where Rome was going with this, but he was going to make Rome spin it out for him. He said, "Go on."

"Well, I figure that then I'd ask us if we was willin' to sort'a quit our jobs."

"But you boys can't quit Tanglewood, can you, Rome?" Slocum said.

Rome considered this. He said, "Well, now, you've got a

point, there, Slocum. We couldn't very well quit our jobs and keep our names. Not if we wanted to live very long. Bass Tanglewood isn't a man to cross."

"So I've heard."

"But then we'd probably say that we wanted to get free more than we wanted to keep our own names."

Slocum began to roll a quirlie. He said, "Doesn't mean much, Rome. Men change names out here like other people change hats back east." He licked at the paper.

"Good point," Rome said with a nod of his head. "Reckon we'd have to do more than change our names, anyhow. Mr. Tanglewood's got awful long arms."

Slocum nodded and struck a match. He drew in the first lungful of smoke before he said, "Sounds like you're up a creek, Rome." He slung his boots up into the seat of the next chair and exhaled a plume of smoke. "And you sorta got me up there with you. I wish somebody had thought to bring a paddle."

London let out a long sigh. "You're gonna kill us anyhow, ain't you?"

Slocum shook his head. "No, London. I'm not." London's relief was palpable. But then Slocum went on, "I'm just tryin' to figure what to do with you. Because if I don't kill you, Tanglewood will. I'm not letting Beth go back to him."

This last sentence was stated with some conviction. He'd seen Beth's back, after all. He wouldn't send a rabid dog or a rank steer back to Bass Tanglewood, let alone a woman.

Even if she was certifiable.

Rome looked at him. "Well, I have to say that I'm kinda with you on that. I don't know what he does to her, but some awful funny noises carry down to the bunkhouse at night."

Slocum just nodded.

"You gonna untie us, then?" London asked. He'd found

out he wasn't going to die, Slocum thought, but now he was pushing it.

"Mayhap in the morning," Slocum said. "You boys will understand if I'm not the most trustin' soul?"

London opened his mouth to complain, but Rome shut him up with a glance and said, "I can sure understand that, yessir I can. Why, we're a couple of desperate fellers, London. Ain't that right, Slocum?"

Slocum took another long drag off his smoke and said, "That you are, Rome."

He looked at Rome, who was the one wearing the black britches. He'd seen just one black-clad leg before he passed out, back up in the trees, and he knew that Rome was the one who had whacked him. He also knew that they probably hadn't even turned him over to look at his face, despite their hints to the contrary.

They hadn't known who he was until he'd introduced himself to Beth back at camp, when they were already tied up.

He said, "When you hit a man over the head, Rome, try to remember that there are places that kill and places that don't. The way I see things, this is sorta all your fault."

Rome gulped. "*My* fault?"

"'Cause you didn't kill me when you stole my horse," Slocum said with no expression.

"Sorry he didn't, too," London piped up.

"What are you doin', you fool?" Rome roared. "You don't apologize to a feller for not killin' him! Jesus. Slocum, don't pay any attention to my little brother, here. He don't have the brains to blow himself up."

Slocum wanted to laugh, but he held it in, and held his lips in a straight, flat line so as not to give himself away. He swore, he'd never seen anything to beat these Granger boys.

Well, there was no way he was going to leave them at liberty tonight. He turned down the lamp and stood up, grinding the stub of his smoke out on the floor.

"You goin' to bed, now?" asked London.

"Yeah, but I ain't goin' upstairs." Slocum hopped up on the bar and stretched out. "I figure to keep you boys company. Hope you don't snore. I'm a real light sleeper."

"Aw, crud," he heard London mutter.

He waited until they both fell asleep in their chairs before he allowed himself to doze off.

At about three in the morning, Beth suddenly sat bolt upright in her bed.

How had she gotten here?

And where was here?

And more important, why was she sleeping in a strange bed, stark naked?

She felt around until she found the stub of a candle, then scraped hands through empty drawers and found a dusty box of sulphurtips. She lit one, and held it to the candle's wick. The room came flickering into view.

Tatty, she thought. Long abandoned and musty. But why was she here? The last thing she remembered was fighting with Slocum on the trail.

Wrapping herself in a bedsheet, the candle in one hand, she let herself out into the hallway, then crept toward the top of the stairs.

The faint glow of a lamp, turned down for the night, barely illuminated the saloon downstairs. She squinted, not wanting to go down into unknown territory, and made out the Grangers. Tied into their chairs, they seemed to be sleeping.

Where was Slocum?

A moment later, the tiny glow of her candle picked out his form, atop the bar. What a strange place to sleep!

She thought about sneaking down and waking him, telling him to come upstairs. But then, her foot on the first tread down, she stopped.

Perhaps he'd already been upstairs. Perhaps he'd already been with her!

She drew her foot back up to the landing and stood there, thinking this over. It was possible, she supposed. She did find him attractive. But something in that attraction had a disabling effect on her, made her go away more often. She'd "been away" more in the last day and a half than she cared to think about.

No, she wouldn't wake him. Let him sleep on the top of the bar. Maybe he had a good reason for it.

Then again, maybe he'd slept with her, then retreated to that hard, wooden surface just to get away from her. Perhaps she'd been horrible to him.

But, he hadn't been horrible to her. She felt no new pains, no new aches, no new insults. Maybe she'd best just let it be until morning.

Softly, she turned and went back down the hall to the room where she'd awakened, her candle's wavering light guiding the way.

13

Dawn broke over an already breakfasted and packed-up Joe French.

He kicked out the embers of his campfire and paused a moment, staring off toward the east. He could see nothing more than gently rolling hills covered by low, sparse vegetation.

That, and a couple of circling hawks or two.

He knew that Slocum and the others were up there, though. And he knew that by nightfall, he'd likely be a rich man.

It was a good feeling.

He stared another second, and then he went over and picked up the gray's reins. He patted it absently on the neck, saying, "Today's the day." He mounted, lowered his hat brim, and started the horse to the east, into the sun, and toward his destiny.

The total transient population of tiny and windswept Cholla was abuzz with activity, too.

Beth had risen, although Slocum had tried to avoid her as much as possible. This was a fairly simple thing to do, because he had plenty on his hands.

He'd decided to cart the Grangers along, although with bound hands. He wasn't going to take any chances. He figured to alert the law, once he got within shouting distance of some, and let them deal with the problem. Also, he had decided not to press charges about Panther's theft.

All things considered, Rome and London Granger couldn't know how impossibly lucky they were.

He'd also decided what to do with Beth Tanglewood.

He knew of a place outside Phoenix, a place where the nuns were kind, and where they had the facilities to care for somebody like Beth. If, indeed, there was anybody else like her. He doubted it. But the Sisters at this particular convent were kind and would understand.

He knew the Mother Superior from way back, when she lived in Mexico. And he also knew she'd accept Beth with open arms and an open heart. It was the best thing he could figure to do with her. He couldn't just turn her loose: There was no telling what kind of trouble she'd find herself in.

If anybody had ever been a real danger to themselves—and to others—it was Beth Tanglewood. She was her own worst enemy. Well, aside from Bass Tanglewood, Slocum thought belatedly. That rich old buzzard must be peach-orchard crazy, too.

After he'd taken care of the Grangers' morning needs and his own, fed and saddled the horses, and refilled all the canteens, he called to Beth.

"We're leaving!" he called from in front of the saloon. A grumpy Rome and a whiney London were already roped onto their horse, which was tied to the rail next to Panther.

There was no response, though.

"Where you reckon she's got to, Rome?" London asked.

"Anybody's guess," Rome replied. "And shut up."

"You're not the boss of me," London said. "Mr. Tanglewood is."

"Both of you, shut your pie holes," growled Slocum and

pushed through the bat-wing doors calling, "Beth? Beth! We're ready to go!"

He was halfway to the staircase when she appeared on the landing. She beamed at him, and then came skipping down the steps. "Good morning!" she said brightly. "I hope I didn't keep you waiting."

"No," Slocum replied warily. "Not at all." And then he offered his arm.

She took it gladly, and walked with him to the doors and out onto the sidewalk. And then stopped cold.

"You!" she suddenly said. To Rome, he thought. And then she turned to London. "And you!"

When she said nothing further, Slocum said, "Beth? You want to get on your horse?"

She turned on him. "Who are you?" she demanded. "What are you doing with them?" She whirled back around and shouted, "You're not going to take me back, not now, not ever!" and took off, running down the street.

"I'm too tired for this crud," Slocum muttered. Shaking his head, he turned Panther loose. "Fetch," he said.

The horse was gone in an instant. Rome and London stared, bug-eyed, as the horse quickly cut off Beth, who came skidding to a halt. Slowly, he then moved her back up the street. The Appaloosa headed off her every escape attempt, bobbed when she bobbed, wove when she wove, and soon had her back down beside Slocum and the Grangers.

"Slocum?" Rome asked, slack-jawed. "How much you want for that horse?"

Slocum ignored him and said, "Up on your bay, Beth. We're going to Phoenix."

She looked dazed, but he didn't have time to fool with her now. She'd be just as liable to be dazed all over again in five minutes, anyway.

"Foot in the stirrup, that's my girl," he said as he gave her a boost up.

He swung up on Panther.

"All right," he said as he dug for his jerky. He'd fed the Grangers, but he hadn't eaten yet. He doubted that Beth had, either. "We're goin' south. Rome and London, you take the lead. Mrs. Tanglewood and I'll follow you. And don't try kicking that nag into a gallop. Your horse is carrying a whole lot of extra weight, and my Panther will round up, cut out, or retrieve anything, and that includes your sorry asses. Got that?"

London nodded and Rome, who was obviously still marveling over what he'd just seen, said, "Got it. How'd you teach that horse to do that?"

They moved forward, the Granger brothers leading the way and Slocum and a pacified Beth bringing up the rear.

"Didn't," Slocum replied as they moved down the street, dodging tumbleweeds as they went. "It's just a natural talent."

Three hours later, Joe French rode cautiously into the ghost town. But he found no people, only the signs that they'd been there, and recently. Two troughs were still half-full of water, there'd been horses in the stable recently, and it looked like somebody over at the saloon had called in a cleaning woman, then pitched a fit in it.

Strange.

But they were all four traveling together this morning— well, only three horses, but he could tell by the depth of the tracks that one was carrying double—and that was stranger still.

He scratched at his graying hair. Those last two had stolen Slocum's horse, so why was he riding with them, all polite, like nothing had happened?

Frankly, he'd expected to find those boys' bodies, not fresh signs of their tracks.

He hadn't told Harley, but he knew who Slocum was, all

right, and from personal experience. They'd ridden to-gether, once upon a time.

Joe and his pals Fredericks and Red had been working on Sam Neill's spread, just south of the Indian Territory, when Slocum hired on. He was supposed to be just another bronc buster, and they hadn't paid him much mind at all. Of course, they were pretty distracted, what with planning to rob the bank in town and all.

Slocum wasn't even his name then! Well, maybe it had always been Slocum, but at the time Joe had known him, he was Frazier, Bill Frazier.

To make a long story short, Joe and Fredericks and Red had held up the bank all right, but all they'd gotten for their trouble was a spray of lead and a whole lot of trouble.

And most all of it came from Slocum.

Why, it had nearly killed Joe's faith in human nature, for Slocum had shown up, under his real name, this time. He'd chased them down, put them in the clink, and two months later, when they escaped, had hunted them down like dogs.

Well, two of them, anyhow. Red and Fredericks had ended up dead. Joe had hightailed it into Indian country and hid out in a cave all winter. He'd almost frozen his feet off during that long, cold season, not to mention nearly starved to death, but at least he'd escaped Slocum's wrath.

And now, here he was, all over again.

He figured Slocum owed him that ten grand he was carrying. That and more.

Joe French intended to take all that he was due.

Bass Tanglewood had waited all morning, but there was still no rider, still no telegram, still no word from those damned Granger brothers. They were supposed to wire him every other day, and they surely would have passed by a couple towns capable of taking a wire since they left Prescott. And Johnson was too lily-livered not to bring a telegram straight out, if one came.

It was troubling.

He stood on the balcony outside his bedroom, staring to the west. If he squinted, he could just see the thin blue line that marked the sea. He knew that if he brought a spy glass up here, he'd have been about to see the surf breaking.

He hated the sea. Except the scent of the sea breeze, at night. He'd grown fond of that for some reason.

But it wasn't night now. He turned on his heel and went back inside, thinking that if he did not hear from them today, he would send a rider into town, to see Johnson. He'd try to backtrack them from their last known position. Maybe a line was down somewhere.

He hoped that Beth hadn't seduced one of the Grangers into letting her go. He would be very unhappy about that, he thought as he strode through his bedroom and to the landing. Very unhappy, indeed.

It would be such a shame to have to kill the Grangers after such a long association.

But Beth was capable of it, when she was in the right mood. And the Grangers, although stalwart in their own way, were certainly capable of bending to her will.

Beth could be very strong-willed at times. In fact, he liked her best when she was defiant, when she was strong.

When she fought him.

Slowly, he started down the wide stairs. He would hate to lose his Beth. At least, he would hate to lose her by any other man's hand than his own.

"Senor Tanglewood?"

He looked down toward the voice, which belonged to Julio, his butler. The man had a face like a funeral, Bass thought. He'd never seen him smile. He said, "Yes, what is it?"

"The governor and Senator Standish have arrived, Senor," Julio said gravely. "They are waiting in the library." Like a tombstone, his face was. Bass wondered if it had frozen that way, and then almost laughed.

And that somber tone only added to the hint that these were important men. Ha! Governor Ruben and Senator Standish?

They were nothing more than employees to Bass Tanglewood, just two more flunkies to be kept waiting on his pleasure.

He said, "Thank you, Julio," rather pleasantly, and straightened his cuffs, then added, "Is it close to the dinner hour?" even though he knew it was.

"Yes, Senor," came the answer.

"Then tell Maria there will be two more to dine," Bass said. "Tell her to make that lemon ice for dessert."

He started down the stairs again, but Julio cleared his throat, as if he wanted to add something.

"Yes, Julio?" Bass asked, one brow hiked.

"I do not think there is time for the lemon ice, Senor," Julio said without expression. "The man with the ice, he does not come until tomorrow."

Bass sighed. "Very well. Whatever she had planned, then."

"Yes, Senor," came the practiced answer.

By the time Bass reached the bottom of the stairs, Julio was gone. Bass went to the big mirror in the grand entryway and straightened his tie, then leisurely buffed his nails against his jacket. If he heard nothing from the Grangers today, he would send someone, probably Donner, tomorrow.

Such a shame.

But it had to be done.

14

"Psst! Rome!"

His voice low, his tone annoyed, Rome replied, "What, London?"

London surreptitiously took a peek over his shoulder, presumably to see if Slocum looked like he was listening. Rome peeked too—he couldn't help it—and saw that Slocum and Mrs. Tanglewood were riding along fairly peaceably about twenty yards back.

In a stage whisper, London continued, "Rome, why don't we just scoot? Hell, he ain't payin' no attention to us!"

Rome shook his head. "Think about it. He's got the rifle, and he's supposed to be a crack shot. Do you know how long it would take us to get out of range, especially ridin' double? Do you know how much quicker we'd be dead before we even got half that far?"

London appeared to consider this, although Rome sometimes thought that he was just pausing to think up a newer, dumber question.

But this time, London's question wasn't dumb.

"Rome?" he asked. "How we gonna get out of this? I mean, you couldn't have been serious about leavin' Mr. Tanglewood!"

"True," Rome said with a nod. "Ain't nobody west of the Mississippi pays like he does. Maybe not east, either. 'Course, it doesn't help that he pays good if he fires us. Or worse."

London nodded solemnly, and lowered his whisper even more. "It's the 'worse' part that I'm worried about, Rome."

"Me, too."

They rode on a little farther, skirting cactus and keeping it down to a walk, as per Slocum's orders. Rome took another quick glance back.

Slocum was holding his distance. It didn't look like he and Mrs. Tanglewood were exactly having a lively conversation back there, either. When they'd first been hog-tied by Slocum, he'd sort of figured Slocum to have a warm spot for Mrs. Tanglewood.

It looked like Slocum had gotten to know her, though. In a nonbiblical sense, that was.

"Maybe tonight," London began, "after he goes to sleep, we can—"

"He don't sleep," interjected Rome with no small degree of disgust. "Least not very hard or deep, not that I can figure. I woke up once last night, and I'd swear he heard my eyelids creak. Picked his damned head up off the bar and said, 'Don't get any ideas.' Like I was plannin' on runnin'!"

"Well, you was, wasn't you?"

Sheepishly, Rome said, "Yeah. But only after I woke you up, London."

"Well, what we gonna do, then?"

"I don't know yet, little brother. I been thinkin' on it all morning."

"Well, I don't like to be rushin' you, Rome," London said, "but could you think a little faster? We ain't that far out of Phoenix."

"Don't I know it."

In fact, this was what concerned Rome the most. If they didn't turn this thing around pretty damned soon, it was going to get a whole lot more tangled up. Hell, it would likely take them a week or more to shake free of the law and track down Mrs. Tanglewood all over again, and longer to get her back from wherever she lit out to and back to the ranch.

Damn that Slocum, anyhow!

Well, in the meantime, he'd just keep pretending that he was going along with Slocum, that everything was just dandy. And London had better do the same, if he knew what was good for him.

Rome had no illusions. He knew Slocum was smarter than he was. He knew that Slocum was a faster hand with a gun and a better long-distance shot than he could ever think to be.

There was only one thing Rome and London did better than anyone, and that was follow the track of man, beast, or otherwise through rain, snow, dust, knee-high mud, flood, and damn near cyclones: a skill that wasn't serving them at all in this situation.

But he hoped that maybe, just maybe, he could be a better liar than Slocum.

He just had to think up the right lie, that was all.

Slocum had been watching most of the little conversation between the Grangers, and he figured he knew what they were talking about: how to fox him.

He figured that he'd be smart to keep them tied, too, and all the way to Phoenix. Of course, they'd have to know that if they took off, he could knock both of them out of their saddles before they got twenty yards.

That's why they were being so agreeable.

So far, anyway.

"What are you going to do with me?" Beth suddenly said. She hadn't spoken for three hours, and it startled him.

"You're gonna be fine," he said, trying to make his voice cheery and uplifting. He didn't want her quirting that bay today and taking off for the horizon, like she had yesterday. "You'll never have to see Bass Tanglewood again if you don't want to."

She was silent, and only a faint nod of her head indicated that she'd heard him.

So they rode on in silence. But Slocum couldn't help but think. He'd got this feeling last night, this feeling that somebody was tailing him.

Stupid idea, he'd told himself. Of course, he was carrying quite a bit of money—to put it mildly—but hell! There had been a bunch of people back in Flagstaff who knew he was carrying it, but there couldn't be anybody else who knew where he'd headed when he'd left town.

He couldn't even think of anybody in this neck of the woods who'd be out to get him. Once again, he went through the list: "Doc" Mertins, in prison over at Yuma; Tinker Phelps, dead; Tommy Kilkullen and Rance Ferber, also deceased, and Tommy at Slocum's hand; Melvin Shoats, doing time up in Wyoming; Christopher Grant, paralyzed during the Mocassin County wars and settled in Santa Fe; Bill "Tonto" Persimmon, over in Yuma, too.

But still, he had that feeling.

It tickled at the back of his brain, nagging him. He'd even glanced over his shoulder once or twice in the past hour. Nobody was there, of course, but he still looked.

Never mind, he told himself. *We'll be in Phoenix in two hours. In Santa Rosa before that.*

Santa Rosa was the little town just outside Phoenix where the Sisters of Mercy had their convent. It was also where he planned to drop off Beth Tanglewood.

So he just sat his horse, kept a cautious eye on the Grangers and Beth, and tried to ignore that itchy feeling. Just two more hours and he'd be shed of the lot of them, and over at Stella's place, in Rosie's arms.

Good old Rosie. Good old simple, uncomplicated, generous Rosie Hammersmith with the big brown eyes and the plump bosom and the willing smile. Despite himself, he smiled just a little.

"Are you laughing at me?" came the imperious question from beside him.

His fingers went to his hat brim. "No, ma'am," he said as seriously as he could, and tipped the brim slightly. "Not at all."

Two more hours.

Jesus.

An hour and a half later, they rode onto the dusty streets of the town of Santa Rosa, population: forty. On a good day.

Slocum headed them toward the steeple of the adobe church with the little, rough sign out front that read SISTERS OF MERCY.

"What now?" joked Rome. "You gonna give us to Jesus?"

"Not you, exactly," Slocum growled.

They stopped out in front, and Slocum hollered, "Hello the church! Anybody home?"

A second later, the front doors opened and a nun poked her head out. "Who goes there what has to holler at the door of God's House instead of coming in?" she called.

"John Slocum, Sister," Slocum replied.

Still, he didn't dismount. He figured not to give Rome and London even the slightest chance to get free of him, especially not where there were buildings they could hide behind.

And a shop they could steal guns from.

"Wonder if I could talk to your Mother Superior, Sister," he continued.

"Come in, then, stranger, and bless you," she said, and moved out the steps, gesturing.

" 'Fraid I can't, Sister," he replied. "Got some prisoners here that can't be trusted."

Rome and London exchanged annoyed glances.

"Very well, then," the nun said. Before she slipped back

inside, Slocum noted that she was young, freckled, and pretty, and had just a hint of reddish hair peeking out at the top of her cowl. She was a novice, too.

They sure don't make nuns the way they used to, he thought. *What ever happened to those fat, motherly types?*

A moment later, the church's doors opened again, and Slocum's face lit up. He tipped his hat. "Afternoon, Mother Grace," he said.

"Slocum?" Mother Superior exclaimed, then "Slocum!" as she ran toward him. He dismounted just as she neared, and he caught her and swung her around in his arms. She was laughing.

"My goodness!" she said when he put her down. "I never thought to see you again! At least, not this soon!" Her gaze swept over his traveling companions. "And who is this you have with you?"

"A lady in need of your kindness and ministrations, Mother Grace," he said, "and a couple of rogues that I'm carting to Phoenix. Bob Treadwell still sheriff?"

"Indeed he is," she said, moving toward Beth's horse. She put her hand up. "Come, my dear. You're very welcome."

Amazingly, Beth got down without protest and accompanied her inside. Mother Grace called back, "You coming, Slocum?" and then she appeared to have a few words with the other nuns, who had peeked out after her, watching.

He was about to say no when two nuns, one of them the red-headed novice, came out the door, toting rifles and looking very serious. "Reckon you can handle 'em, ladies?" he asked.

"Sir, I can nail a quail at two hundred yards," said the little red-headed nun. "And I have shot a passel of Apache in my time," she added.

And then she turned toward Rome and London. "You boys want to climb down and let that poor animal you're ridin' have some ease as well as some fresh-drawn water?"

• • •

In the Mother Superior's office—which was little more than a glorified closet, Slocum noticed—he sat across the small desk from Mother Grace.

He'd known her long ago, back in Mexico, when her name was Maria Costello Gomez O'Bannon. Her mother had been half Mexican and half Yaqui Indian with a temper to match, and her father had been pure Irish.

She took more after the Irish side of the family, and before his death, her papa had been one of the best friends that Slocum had ever had.

"I still find myself wanting to call you Uncle," she said with a smile.

"Well," he said with a wink, "I appreciate your restraint. You're all grown up now, too grown up if you were to ask me. You don't want to make me feel old, do you?"

She chuckled. "I doubt that's possible. What's the deal with this lady of yours, Slocum?"

"Thought she was your kind of case. If she's anybody's kind of case." He shook his head. "I ain't never seen nothing like it, Maria. I mean, Mother Grace. It's like she's a whole bunch of different people, and I can never figure out which one I'm talkin' to. It's downright eerie. She's got bad problems at home, too," he added, leaning across the desk.

"As if she didn't have enough already," said Mother Grace in her "tut-tut" tone, and one side of Slocum's mouth twitched up into a slight smile. She'd had that air about her even as a teenager.

"Being brought into this pitiful excuse for a convent by a known felon with two prisoners, for example," she continued with a grin. "How many crimes and misdemeanors are you wanted for at present, Slocum?"

He put his hand on his chest. "Nothing, Mother Grace, nothing at all, I swear. Right at the moment, that is."

She chuckled again.

"I'll take you at your word, Slocum," she said, and

threw him a wink. "Now, tell me about this poor woman."

"Her name is Beth. Beth Tanglewood," he began.

Outside, Rome and London slouched in the shade of a saguaro rib ramada, near their drowsing horse. Sister Agnes, who had shot herself a passel of Apaches, or so she said, stood over them with a rifle.

She looked like she had a mean streak, all right, and Rome was inclined to believe her about those Indians.

But it was good to have some time to get off his horse, sit down on something that wasn't moving, and have a good think. He'd been thinking all right, and he couldn't see a way out of this. Which was bad, because he knew that London expected it of him. Hell, he expected it of himself.

So he was putting all his hopes into the "happy accident" way of thinking: Something would happen on the trail, on the way into Phoenix, he'd decided. Something would happen, and Slocum would get distracted. Just for a second. It wouldn't take long.

He hoped.

"Rome?" asked London quietly. He'd hushed up for almost twenty minutes, Rome decided. That was a pretty long time for London.

So he replied, "What is it?" in a fairly civil tone.

"I been thinkin'," London said softly, "and I can't figure my way out of this deal for beans. You doin' any better?"

It was too late to lie. Rome said, "Not much, little brother. I reckon we'll just hope he makes a mistake on the trail."

"You don't give a feller a lot of hope, Rome," London said.

"Sorry."

Rome didn't hear the shot.

All he saw was the sudden, tiny explosion of blood from his brother's chest. He watched as London sat forward, his eyes glazed, then slouched to the side, dead. "London?" he said. "London?"

Sister Agnes said, "Move!" and he moved, by God.

He practically dove toward the church, toward those big front doors, and saw the kick-up from a slug on either side of him.

As if he needed any more incentive, he felt the barrel of a rifle prod his back.

He picked up speed.

The other nun had rushed through before him, but he was close on her black-clad tail, and Sister Agnes brought up the rear. She slammed the door behind him and cried, "Mother! Mother! Someone's shooting at us!"

15

Joe French lay on his belly on a hill more than three hundred yards from the churchyard, and cursed himself for missing those last two shots.

At least the first one had been good. The body lay in a little heap, not moving, still as death.

Still as death: That was a good one, he thought with a smirk.

He'd loped and jogged then loped again, easily making time on Slocum and his party, who were traveling at a walk, judging from their tracks. Actually, he'd been within range for some time, and thanked his lucky stars that they'd decided to pull into Santa Rosa. Finding a spot where they'd be in the open—but he'd have cover—would have been a job, otherwise.

Now that they were all inside, it would just be a waiting game, he mused, softly blowing an infinitesimal layer of dust from his telescopic rifle sights.

He carefully lay the rifle beside him. He'd be fine. He could wait them out. He had the shade of a lone palo verde, plenty of food and water and extra water and feed for his horse, which was staked out of sight, just behind the crest of the low hill.

He could wait for days.

Which was several days longer than old Slocum would be able to stand it, if he knew Slocum. And he thought he did.

He wouldn't have gone down there to face Slocum. He wouldn't have faced off with him anywhere. He wasn't that much of a fool.

But at a distance?

That was different.

It had occurred to him that he might have to kill a whole passel of nuns to get to that ten thousand that Slocum was carrying, but then, he'd done worse in his time, hadn't he?

He couldn't say that it bothered him. Nothing much did. Nothing but being poor, that was, and he was about to become a rich man.

He smiled, and waited.

At Slocum's order, all the nuns pulled the open shutters closed with a reverberating *bang-bang-bang* as he grabbed Rome by the collar. "Where'd the shots come from?" he demanded.

Rome, belatedly dazed, just stared at him. Slocum dropped him and turned to the red-headed sister. "Which way?" he shouted.

The sister pointed to the northeast wall of the chapel, and said, "We didn't even hear the shots."

When Slocum arched a brow, she added, "There were at least two more. They missed us. I saw the dust they raised."

"Sister Agnes?" said Rome, who had fallen all the way to the floor when Slocum released him.

She went to him and helped him up, while he said, "Slocum, won't you—?" while he held forward his bound hands.

"Sit down," Slocum snarled.

Rome slumped into a pew.

"How many nuns you got here?" he asked Mother Grace. He knew she was good with a gun, at least, if only he could talk her into using one. Too bad his extras were outside, on Panther.

"Just what you see," she said, and her mouth was set into a hard line. "Just Sisters Agnes, Naomi, Dominique, and myself."

Slocum pegged Naomi and Agnes as the two who had been outside, watching the Grangers. Sister Dominique, a middle-aged, plump woman, was the one who'd spirited Beth off when they first came in. Beth, however, was nowhere in sight.

"No priest?"

"Father Marcus comes once a month," Mother Grace said. "He's not due for another three weeks. Sister Dominique, do we still have that old Henry rifle?"

"Yes, Mother," came the reply, and Slocum suddenly felt a little better. But then, a little tearily, she added, "There are only two bullets left, though. It's my fault. I should have gone to Pedro Mondragon's store and bought more when our supply grew low."

Slocum's heart sank, but not for long. Panther. Had anyone tied him?

He was halfway to the front door when one of the shutters was pierced. Splinters flew as Sister Naomi, who had been standing directly before it and beside Mother Grace, suddenly took one faltering step forward, eyes blinking rapidly, whispered, "My God!" and slumped forward, to her knees.

Mother Grace, her check and arm full of splinters, caught her before she toppled all the way to the floor and cradled her in her arms. Beseechingly, she looked up at Slocum.

Slocum didn't way a word. He turned back to the door and opened it. At least he was sure where the shots were coming from, now. And the shooter had to be using a scope. He had to be a long way off for them not to hear the shots, and he had to be an ace with that rifle.

Panther, he saw, wasn't tied. He was stuck in a corral, but still saddled and bridled. For half a second he was about to lecture the sisters about turning out a tacked-up horse, then remembered himself.

He whistled.

Panther's head came up from his hay, ears pricked.

Slocum whistled again.

This time, Panther walked to the closed gate and nudged it with his nose.

Slocum swore softly, under his breath, then whistled again, loudly.

This time, Panther seemed to understand what he wanted. He trotted back to the opposite side of the small paddock, turned around again, paused, eyed the gate, then sprang into a canter.

He cleared the fence easily, trotted over, and when Slocum opened the second door, came right up into the building, ducking to avoid the door's frame. He whickered softly, and looked around him.

"Christ almighty, Slocum!" Rome said.

"Sir!" snapped Sister Agnes, who was helping Mother Grace with Sister Naomi. "You're in a house of God!" Sister Agnes, while not hurt seriously, was bleeding from her face.

Rome acted as if he hadn't heard her, and just kept staring at the horse.

Slocum barely noticed this though. He started taking weapons and ammunition from Panther's saddlebags and boot. "Hope you don't mind," he said as he worked, piling his and the Grangers' firearms in the back pew.

"Horses are God's creatures, too," allowed Mother Grace. She and Sister Agnes stood, Sister Naomi between them. She looked to be conscious.

"She gonna be all right?" he asked.

"She'll survive," Mother Grace said.

"You'd best pull those splinters out," Slocum added as

they helped her away, through the back hall and the cells and office.

"Yes, Uncle John," he heard her say before she disappeared around the corner of the hall, and he smiled briefly.

"Uncle John?" asked Rome, his brows arched.

"Shut up," explained Slocum.

"Mr. Slocum, what do you wish me to do?" piped up Sister Dominique. For the first time, Slocum noticed a hint of a French lilt tickling at her stern voice.

"Ma'am," he said as he took stock of his weapons, "I'd appreciate it if you could stay with Mrs. Tanglewood. She's a might . . . jumpy."

He just heard a mumbled, "In more ways than one!" as Sister Dominique followed the others down the hall.

Rome, having pushed his brother's untimely death to the back of his mind—for now, at least—looked expectantly at Slocum. *Untie me, you sonofabitch!* he thought over and over, like a mantra.

But Slocum was paying him little mind.

Rome watched anxiously as Slocum went through boxes of ammunition—both his, and Rome's and London's.

And then Slocum looked up just as another slug came bursting through the shuttered windows. This one went across the open expanse of the church and shattered an icon of the baby Jesus and Mary.

"That bastard ain't got no reverence at all, does he?" Rome mumbled.

"Doesn't appear that way," said Slocum, walking over to him. "Hold out your hands."

Rome did, as fast as he could.

Slocum, the pocketknife already in his hand, said, "I'm trustin' you, Rome. Not all the way, mind, but I'm trustin' you to help protect these women. And your own ornery hide."

"And you, too," Rome replied with a nod. "I get you."

"You'd better," said Slocum, and cut the ropes.

• • •

Joe French was on the move. He'd thought better of staying in one place, and quietly begun leading his horse to another hill, one at more of an angle to the church. From there, he'd be able to shoot at both the side windows and the front door. It would be at an angle, of course, but that only meant that they'd have a harder time getting a bead on his location.

Actually, they hadn't returned his fire. Not once.

He thought this was a little curious.

Maybe Slocum was having a hard time getting all those nuns corralled. How many were they, he wondered. Ten at the most—the place wasn't big enough to hold more than that. And then he wondered if he'd killed Slocum when he'd fired through the shutters. Now, that would surely be a lucky break!

He wasn't counting on it, though. It would be just Slocum's luck to avoid anything so happenstance as a blind shot.

Also curious was that damned horse going right in the front door of the church! In fact, he'd been in such shock that he hadn't thought to shoot. At least, not until he realized that the Appy was likely carrying more guns and ammunition, and by then, it was too late.

At last he came to the perfect spot. He staked out his horse, grabbed his rifle and canteen and another box of ammunition, and crawled up to the top of another gentle hill.

He peered over the top.

Good. The church was in full view, and he'd gone far enough that the few squat buildings that comprised the town weren't in the way.

He seemed to have cleared the streets. There wasn't one human in evidence. He sat up a little farther and squinted toward the ramada, then gave up and looked through his rifle's telescopic sight. There was the body, still there.

They'd made no attempt to retrieve it while he wasn't looking.

He swung the rifle over toward the church itself. The front windows were a tad battered, courtesy of his bullets, and he snickered under his breath.

He was just moving the rifle, and its sight, over to the front doors when a slug splatted into the ground, not a foot from him!

As he quickly backed down the hill, his hair standing on end, he saw the front door open. And pulled the trigger. Once with hope, and once out of sheer frustration when it slammed shut.

Damn that Slocum!

16

Slocum pulled back from the doorway just before it was hit by an answering round. He wished he had a telescopic sight. The only reason he'd even known where the shot came from was the tiniest hint of a puff of smoke that rose a second before the slug hit the open door, inches from his shoulder.

What kind of a lunatic would be out there, anyhow? There was no water for miles, save for the well here in Santa Rosa. There was hardly any cover to shield a man from the sun or the wind or the rain.

His back against the wall, next to the closed, splintered door, he sighed. The point was that the man was out there. Slocum figured it to be one man, anyway. Two would have come at them from opposite sides, and at the same time.

But this one had fired from one position, then moved before he fired those last two shots into the front of the church.

At least, Slocum was pretty damned sure that he had.

He searched the walls until he found where a slug aimed at him had gone home, and then, while he dug it out of the adobe, he said, "Rome?" He nodded to the place where, earlier, the icon had been shattered. "See if you can dig that slug outta the wall."

Rome, newly equipped with his rifle and gun, said, "Sure thing."

Rome appeared to be a bit perkier than before, although he was still moving a little slowly. Slocum figured that if it was his brother who'd just been killed, he'd be moving slowly, too.

At last, Slocum freed the bullet. A second later, Rome found his, too.

"Gimme that," Slocum said, and held the bullets up, side by side.

Same caliber.

Could be the same gun.

He slowly turned both slugs in his hands, and saw that one had a very fine scratch up and down its length. Odd. Of course, it could have come from hitting the wall, running into a little rock in the adobe.

But then he found the same tiny scratch on the second slug. There weren't any rocks in the door, and it sure wasn't likely that it, too, had hit a pebble in the wall that left the same, identical pattern.

They were from the same gun, all right.

He stuck the slugs in his pocket and said to Rome, "We've only got one shooter out there."

Rome just stared at him.

Mother Grace appeared in the hallway door. "It wasn't bad," she said. "Sister Naomi will be right as rain, thank the Lord."

"How's Beth?" asked Slocum.

"She's resting quietly," came the answer. "Sister Dominique gave her some tea laced with laudanum. Put her right to sleep."

"Good," said Slocum with a grunt. The last thing he needed was Beth Tanglewood throwing one of her fits during a fire fight, but he hadn't heard a single peep out of her since they'd arrived and Sister Dominique hustled her off. "She sure must have doctored that tea heavy."

Mother Grace smiled a little. "Sister Dominique is not known for half-measures. In anything." She entered the church, stuck her hands into the deep folds of her sleeves, and sat primly in one of the pews.

Could this possibly be the teenager he'd taught to play baseball? That he'd admired in her first-communion dress and given pesos to, for candy?

Probably fifteen years had passed since that last visit, he remembered. And out here, the Catholic Church had to promote fast.

Mother Grace. He found himself continually amazed.

"What now, Slocum?" she asked.

He knew her well enough to figure that she meant, "What did you bring down on our heads this time, you sonofabitching bastard?"

He was glad she'd become a nun. Anyhow, it had sure cleaned up her language.

He said, quite honestly, "I don't know, Mother Grace. But there's only one feller out there, according to my calculations."

Rome, who had remained quiet up until now, nodded his head and said, "Yes, ma'am, just one."

Slocum hauled back his hand, as if to strike him, and Rome cowered.

"Now, gentlemen . . ." purred Mother Grace, ever the diplomat. "Do you have a plan, Slocum?"

Slocum pulled out his pocket watch and peered at it. It was a quarter past five. He said, "We'll keep an eye on his last known position till dark, Mother. And then I'm gonna try to get round behind him."

Mother Grace hiked a brow. "On foot?"

"'Course not," Slocum replied, and hiked a thumb toward Panther, who was still standing in a corner of the room.

As if on command, the gelding lifted his broomy tail and deposited a number of fresh, pungent road apples on the floor, then let loose with a long jet of gas.

Slocum, Mother Grace, and Rome watched in silence until Panther was finished, and then Mother Grace said, "Just how long till it gets dark, Slocum?"

Beth Tanglewood drowsed, uneasily tossing on the edge of sleep.

Sometimes, she was aware of a women—a nun?—nearby. Why would there be a nun? But why would anybody else dress all in black?

Sometimes, she half imagined she was on the trail with Slocum, and then it turned into Andy, when she was fourteen and innocent.

Then it turned into something strange, something she didn't recognize, couldn't recognize, and then, mercifully, she "went away" again.

When she awakened, it was nearly dark outside. The beams of sunlight that had been filtering through the closed shutters in the little room were almost nonexistent, and the nun—there *was* a nun!—was lighting a row of squat, white candles on a shelf across the room.

The nun turned toward her in the tiny room, which couldn't have been more than eight feet by six.

"You're awake, then!" the nun said in a pleasant voice. She left the candles and sat in a wicker chair next to the bed. She patted Beth's hand. "And how are you feeling, my dear?"

"Where am I?" Beth asked. The last thing she remembered was waking up in the saloon and seeing Slocum downstairs, asleep on the top of the bar. She said, "This isn't a bar, is it? Why would there be a nun in a saloon?"

The nun took no offense at this question and said, "You're safe, *mon petite chou*. I'm Sister Dominique, and you're with the Sisters of Mercy. Mr. Slocum brought you. Do you remember?"

Beth shook her head, trying to clear it. Had they given

her something? She felt so . . . foggy. "Not really. Where and what is the Sisters of Mercy?"

"The *where* is just outside Phoenix," replied Sister Dominique in the same mild, caring tone. "In the town of Santa Rosa, to be precise. The *what* takes longer to explain."

Slowly, Beth boosted herself into a sit. "I have time, Sister," she said, rather groggily. "At least, I think I do. Go ahead. Tell me."

Out in the church proper, having already cleaned up after the horse—twice—Slocum was tightening Panther's girth. The sun would be all the way down in the next few minutes, and he wasn't going to waste any time.

"Easy, boy," he muttered. "Easy, Panther. In just a shake you'll be able to shit all you want without anybody pitching a fit."

Rome, who had been sitting back in the corner of the dim room, snorted. Slocum had tied him up again, since he didn't trust him out of his sight.

"Don't light any candles or lanterns till you hear Panther's hoof beats fade," Slocum said.

Mother Grace, waiting quietly in a nearby pew, her face bandaged, nodded through the dying light.

"I don't believe God minds a little horse manure, Slocum," she said. "After all, His son was born in a stable."

"Yeah," Slocum said, and Mother Grace smiled.

"I'm gonna leave you Rome's handgun," Slocum went on. "If that jackass out there decides to sneak up on you, or if he gets me before I get him, you'll need all the guns you can get."

"Amen and amen," said Rome. The sound echoed slightly.

"Now, let's not be insulting to jackasses," Mother Grace said, and stood up.

She came close to him, ducking under Panther's neck.

To Slocum, she whispered softly, "You still want us to do . . . the other? As we discussed earlier?"

Slocum nodded. He and Mother Grace had had themselves quite a private conversation after the last bullet had splintered the front door.

"Yeah," he said, and glanced again at the shutters. Nothing was coming through them at the moment except the black of a night sky. "You're sure you all can handle it?"

"Don't be absurd, Slocum." She winked at him then, and he knew she was capable.

"All right," he said, loudly enough so that Rome could hear him, too. "It's time. Everybody, remember what you're supposed to do," he added, mostly to Mother Grace.

She said, "God bless you, Slocum."

Sister Agnes, who had been caring for Sister Naomi, emerged from the hall. A candle flickering softly in her hand, she said, "Yes, Slocum. Bless you. Now, go with God."

She blew out the candle's flame and Slocum led Panther toward the front doors.

Mother Grace stood there, her hand on the latch. "Ready?" she asked.

"Ready," Slocum said.

She threw open both doors. Slocum, hunkered down in the saddle, propelled Panther through the opening and out, into the night.

He reined a hard right around the side of the church, out of the sniper's sight—he hoped—and cantered away. The plan was to come around behind him, and Slocum figured the best way to do that was to cut way back, to the west.

Once he made to the far side of those low hills, finding the sniper would be fairly easy, even with just a half moon.

Slocum was in his element. After all, he was now the hunter, not the hunted.

In an odd way, Slocum was actually looking forward to

seeing his face. He wanted to know who the hell was so keen on killing him.

Joe French had been waiting for nightfall, too.

His rifle sight wasn't any good at night, but he knew where he was going.

When it was time, he slung his rifle over his shoulder, saddled his gray again, and carefully, quietly, began to lead it over the hill.

Down there was Slocum and his bankroll.

Down there was Joe's future.

And he was going to claim it—no matter what it took.

17

Bass Tanglewood waited in the dark, on his front porch, for Donner to ride in. Donner had been sent to town to check with the telegrapher's office, to see if the lines were down between there and Prescott.

The Grangers still hadn't wired. This worried Bass, but it also enraged him.

And so, giving the Grangers the benefit of the doubt, he'd sent Donner into town.

Now, Donner wasn't the sort that most men sent off on an errand, and he hadn't been too pleased about it. Donner was a hired gun, the best in the business. Tanglewood kept him on the payroll for . . . special assignments.

Bass Tanglewood stared past the outbuildings, past the corrals, through the darkness toward the road to Los Angeles. Any minute, he kept telling himself. Any minute.

When Donner finally did ride in, he came at a slow jog, and he didn't have good news. He dismounted, casually tossed his reins over the rail, and pulled up a chair opposite Tanglewood's.

"Wires ain't down," Donner said, lighting a slim, black cigarette. He was a tall man, dark blond and clean-shaven, with an aquiline nose and narrow blue eyes. His lips were permanently set in a hard, straight line. As with Julio the butler, Tanglewood didn't believe he'd ever seen him smile.

"We tried every place between here and Prescott," Donner went on, "and everybody wired back. Also wired back that they ain't had no trouble with the lines." He looked toward the front door and licked his lips.

Tanglewood turned his head and bellowed, "Maria! Bring the whiskey!" Then he turned again to Donner.

"You leave in the morning," he said calmly. "First thing. I want you to find those two idiots. And not incidentally, my wife."

Donner nodded.

Just then the screen banged open and out came Maria, bearing a decanter and two glasses. "Don't shout for me," she said to Tanglewood. "You're old. It is bad for your heart."

Tanglewood grunted and waved her away. "Get back to the goddamn kitchen. Harridan! And there's nothing wrong with my damned heart!"

She paused at the screen door. "It is no skin off my nose if you wish to die. My sister, Conchita, has a place for me in her home."

"Go!" shouted Tanglewood, and he muttered, "Goddamn women!" after the screen banged shut behind her. "I'd take a quirt to her, 'cept it wouldn't be worth the trouble."

"Huh?" said Donner.

"Nothing. Never mind."

Slocum had reached a point about three-quarters of a mile from the place he was assuming was their sniper's position, and he was carefully making his way forward. There was no telling what this idiot was going to do next.

All the while he rode, Slocum racked his brain for possible snipers. He supposed it could be Kinsey Langham, except the last he heard, Langham was up in Canada. He supposed it could have been Chance Mulroney, but Chance was still working the poker tables up around Seattle, and besides, Slocum's taking him at a night of poker was hardly worth traveling all this way to try to kill him.

He went through a dozen names, each one both newly thought of and with a grudge just as ancient, but every single one of them was out of the territory or in jail or dead.

Shit.

At last, he came to the place where the final shots had come from, and found a lone palo verde, a place where a horse had stood for a long time, and the scuff marks where a man had skinnied up the slope and lay on his belly.

He also found a rifle casing, which was the same caliber as the slugs they'd dug from the interior walls of the church.

He shook his head. Who the hell was this guy?

And then he began to widen his mental search. Maybe this yahoo wasn't after him at all. Maybe it was somebody after the Grangers, or Beth Tanglewood.

That sure opened up a whole new can of worms, didn't it? Hell, if the idea that somebody wanted Rome had come to him a little sooner, he would have just pushed Rome out the front door.

Well, no. He wouldn't have. But it was a nice thought.

While Slocum was just getting to the low range of hills, about to start creeping east again, Beth sat up.

She was still groggy, but she was awake enough to see her chance. Sister Dominique, lulled into a sense of security by Beth's feigned sleep, had taken a well-deserved break. She'd tiptoed out the door, quietly latched it behind her, and been gone nearly five minutes.

Probably to have some dinner.

So Beth stood herself up, straightened her dress, and carefully unlatched the shutters.

It was dark out, but it wasn't a long drop to the ground.

She eased herself out and had walked twenty feet before she realized that she had no food, no gear, and most important, no horse.

She stopped stock still, cursing herself for being such an idiot. Now, where would they keep the horses?

Not here. All she could see ahead was a vast plain, rimmed by low hills.

The stable must be around the other side.

She retraced her steps, then hugged the building. Around the corner she crept, making as little noise as possible, then around another corner. Ahead she saw a small corral and a ramada, picked out by the moon. And there was a horse in the ramada—her bay, in fact!—saddled and bridled, as if the gelding were waiting for her!

No one came out of the church when she crept to the corral and quietly opened the gate.

No one so much as cracked a door or a closed shutter when she mounted the bay.

And no one came out when she quietly rode the gelding out and skirted the side of the church, then cut across the yard.

She waited until she was a good half mile before she broke into a canter, and headed east. Or at least, what she thought was east.

Away from Bass Tanglewood and toward . . . Well, she wasn't sure what. But anything was better than going back.

Slocum had decided that the rider had gone up and over the hill, and was headed toward the church. But before he could hit the crest of the hill, he reined up Panther, for the distant approach of hoofbeats had come to his ears. Then he realized that they were headed past him, going northeast.

He nudged Panther into a lope, then a full-out run. Besides him, nobody else was out here but the sniper. Slocum didn't know how the man had gotten clear over there, or why he was riding so fast, but he was, by God, going to get the sonofabitch!

Halfway to the church, Joe French, too, heard the rider coming. As fast as he could, he and his horse scurried behind the meager cover of a clump of prickly pear.

Joe brought out his rifle and squatted on one knee.

He had the rider in his sights, but didn't shoot. Was it a woman? Yes, and in a green dress that fluttered out behind her, if the moon wasn't playing tricks on him! She looked to be heading for nothing but the New Mexico border, and she was running her horse flat out. She didn't seem aware of Joe's presence, either.

So he simply waited—the rifle to his shoulder, naturally—while she passed within thirty feet of him, then sped on to the northeast, toward the hills he'd left behind.

Slowly, he lowered his rifle, then shook his head. It was the damnedest thing he'd ever seen.

When the rider came barreling over the crest of the hill, Slocum was ready. He didn't think, he just acted.

He sprang from Panther's back and onto the bay, pushing himself and the rider clear of the saddle and down to the ground. He'd found it was always best to land on the other rider. Otherwise, you got the air knocked out of you and weren't worth a damn for a minute or so.

As the horses loped on, Slocum rose up from the ground and looked down into the face of . . . Beth?

"Aw, shit," he muttered as he pulled her to her feet. She was trying desperately to get the air back into her lungs, and Slocum gave her a thump on the back.

She took in air with a long wheeze, and doubled over, her hands on her knees while she learned how to breath again.

"You pass anybody on your way out?" he demanded.

She didn't answer, only shook her head.

"Nobody at all?"

She stood up. "I told you, sir, no. Who are you, anyway, and why did you push me off my horse? I'll sue you!"

Slocum rolled his eyes and thought *here we go again*, but said, "Calm down, Beth."

He could just make out Panther in the distance. He'd already headed off the bay and was bringing him back. And without being asked!

Good old Panther. If only he could count on Beth a quarter as much!

"I demand you tell me where we are!" she said, and gave a little stomp of her foot.

"Don't you know?"

"I most certainly do not," she said, her arms crossed snugly over her ample bosom. "In fact, I have no idea. Have you kidnapped me, sir?"

"Lady," Slocum said as Panther approached and he took hold of both horses' reins, "You got yourself out here. I'm just tryin' to save you from yourself. Along with a few other things. Now, mount up."

She didn't move. "I only have your word for that, Mr. . . . ?"

"Slocum," he said wearily. "Just plain Slocum."

Somewhere behind her was their sniper. She'd likely been so intent on getting away that if there'd been an elephant out there, she would have ridden right past it, oblivious.

"Get up," he repeated.

When she simply stood there, a defiant look on her pretty face, he said, "Have it your own way."

He mounted Panther, grabbed hold of the bay's reins, and moved on without her.

"Wait!" she called.

He paid her no mind. She'd be safer out here than with him. He could always pick her up later. Or if he couldn't, she'd find her way back to the church. Either way, for the moment she was safer than he was, or Rome, or those nuns down there.

He clucked to the horses, leaving her behind, on the far side of the hill, to scream at him.

Joe reached the ramada, and tied his horse to the back rail. Only the faintest light leaked through the closed shutters and door of the church. The whole town, its few citizens included, seemed to be holding its breath.

Quietly, he pulled down his rifle. He jammed spare ammunition into his pockets—for both his rifle and his sidearm.

He didn't care if he had to shoot his way through everybody in the damned church. Slocum's money was going to be his, by God, and no one was going to talk him out of it.

He crept up to the building, rifle in hand and began working his way around it, looking for the best way inside.

It wasn't long before he found Beth's open window.

18

Once Slocum backtracked a little, he found the sniper's trail.

One man, on foot, leading a horse. Sometimes Slocum moved at a jog; the prints were that clear in the moonlight. Other times, he had to strain to see the trail at all.

One thing had become increasingly apparent, though. The sniper was headed straight for the church.

Beth's cries of outrage had long since faded to nothing behind him. She was safe, at least. He had to make his move now: Either keep carefully tracking this bastard, or take a chance and gallop straight to the church.

He chose the latter.

When he reached the town, though, he pulled up Panther behind the little blacksmith's shed. The horse came to a sliding stop. Slocum leapt off, carrying his rifle in one hand, and darted between the shed and the next squat building. Panther wandered off toward the little pen behind the building, where there were a few startled goats.

Slocum figured staring at them and trying to figure out how to get in there and herd them around would keep the horse busy for a while.

Leaving Panther to his own devices, Slocum crept along

the wall toward the street, sidearm drawn and his rifle in his left hand, until he could peek around the corner.

Shit.

There was a new horse, barely seen, tied back underneath the ramada beside Rome and London's horse, who wasn't tied, but stayed simply for the hay, Slocum supposed. The sniper was here, somewhere in town. And most likely, in the church.

"Psst! Senor!"

Slocum whipped around, gun aimed out.

A small Mexican man stood inside the open window, his hands up. "D-don't shot, senor!" he hissed. "I am Diego Gomez. I live here."

Slocum lowered his gun and waited.

"Senor, what is happening?" Diego continued in a whisper. "We saw you come in before, with the others. My wife and I, we saw Mother Grace greet you. Why is there now all this shooting? Why does the lady ride out so fast, and then the strange man ride in? We heard screams, senor, from the church!"

Slocum stiffened. "How long ago did you hear the screams?"

Diego said, "Right after the man rides in. Maybe a half hour ago." He lowered his voice even further, until Slocum could barely hear him. "Senor, you brought in prisoners. Is this your trouble?"

"Damned if I know, Diego," Slocum answered truthfully.

"Well, my wife and I, we wish you would fix it, or tell us what we can do to help you," Diego said, and Slocum believed he was sincere. "We are most fond of the sisters, senor."

"So am I," Slocum said. "You can be the most help by just stayin' inside, Diego, and outta the way." He turned and started back toward the front corner of the building, and the dusty street.

"Senor!" came the hiss once again. "What is your name?"

"Slocum," he whispered back, then ducked around to the front and cut quickly across the street.

Beth didn't know where she was or how she'd gotten there. She looked around, confused and bewildered. Desert, nothing but desert. Her throat was sore, as if she'd been yelling or screaming or maybe singing for hours on end, and she was thirsty.

She looked down at herself. She recognized her dress. That was one good thing, anyway. Very often, when she lost time, she didn't. It was as if she were wearing a stranger's wardrobe.

And everything was so quiet! There was no sound save for the soft desert breeze and the occasional scuttle of some small, nocturnal, desert-dwelling animal.

She was at the base of a hill, it seemed. She looked to the east and the west, and then decided that no, it was a series of low hills. There was nothing but a vast expanse of nothing to the north.

She picked up her skirts at the knee and began to trudge clumsily up the hill. Perhaps, once she gained the top, she would be able to see something, some sign of civilization.

"I said to stop it, Sister," Joe growled. "Stop it, or you'll get what your friend got."

"Christ blesses even pigs like you," Mother Grace said defiantly, and set the heavy pot down. She should have known better than to try sneaking up behind him.

She should have remembered her place.

She should be praying for him right now.

But somehow, she couldn't bring herself to do it, may God forgive her. He had split poor Sister Dominique's skull in the back hall. It was her scream that had alerted them to his presence. And right now, an unconscious Sister Dominique was on a cot next to Sister Naomi, up by the altar. She had lost so much blood! Sister Agnes was attending to them both.

But Mother Grace had a more proactive attitude than perhaps she should. She had, for the second time, tried to sneak up behind this interloper, this attacker of the Brides of Christ, this invader of God's house.

And for the second time, she'd been caught in the act.

"Get back up there and sit down," barked the man who'd simply said his name was Joe. He wiggled his pistol at her. "Get back. With him."

She grudgingly retreated and sat next to Rome. He had done nothing to help them, nothing to help himself. In fact, he seemed to be actually enjoying this! Well, let him enjoy it, she thought. He was as much in peril as they were.

His hands were tied, after all.

She thought about trying to free him, once upon a time. But no more. They were safer in the hands of one armed man than two.

Again, she wondered about Slocum. Where was he? And where was Beth? Mother Grace hadn't known she was missing until they'd run in to find Sister Dominique lying in her own pooling blood. And Joe, standing over her in the doorway to Beth's empty room. The window shutters had been open wide, and there was no telling how long she'd been gone.

Right then, there was only Joe, a scowl on his face and a gun in each hand, and Sister Dominique.

Dear Lord, she silently prayed, *let her live. She is so good and kind, much better than this humble servant. Let Sister Dominique live, and take me instead.*

She wanted to add, *and take this evil sonofabitch right along with me, and send him down to hell where he belongs,* but resisted that temptation.

And all the time, she kept straining her ears, hoping for the sound of Slocum's returning hoofbeats.

She folded her arms, slid her hands inside the opposing sleeves, and waited.

Joe, too, had been listening for the sound of hoofbeats.

In fact, he thought he'd heard some, just faintly, just before that damned nun had nearly caved in his skull. But now, there was nothing. When he'd turned back to the window, there had been no one, nothing, only the wind and a darkened street.

He guessed he'd imagined it.

Wishful thinking.

He knew Slocum's coming back was a certainty, though. A man like Slocum didn't ride off and leave a prisoner. A man like Slocum didn't ride off and leave him in the hands of a bunch of nuns, anyway.

No, he'd be back. It was just a matter of time.

He turned to make sure that nun wasn't trying anything funny, and saw her sitting there on the edge of that little stage up front, or whatever it was you called it—where the priest stood while he was preaching, he supposed.

Of course, he didn't much care. All he wanted was for her to stay put and shut up.

He glanced outside again. Still clear. Where the hell was Slocum?

He sighed, and turned toward . . . what was his name? He'd asked when he first burst in, once he got the nuns calmed down. The name of some city in the old country. Paris, maybe?

No, Rome. That was it.

He said, "Rome," and the fellow looked up. That nun looked up at him, too. They called themselves the Sisters of Mercy, but, hell, if looks could kill. . . .

He snorted, then asked, "Why you hog-tied?"

Rome, who had the longest, ugliest facial scar that Joe had seen since he'd left old Rye Ticker's place up in the mountains, said, "Guess they don't like me or somethin'."

"Figured that much," Joe said. "How'd you get that scar?"

"Cougar jumped me when I was six," Rome replied, and appeared amazed that somebody had bothered to ask.

Joe hadn't really cared, but he said, "Oh. Only man I ever saw with a scar worse than that got slashed by a grizzly. Just wondered."

Rome appeared vaguely disappointed for some reason that Joe didn't fathom. But once again, he didn't care enough to do more than note it, then forget it. He looked out through the crack in the shutters again.

Nothing.

That sonofabitch Slocum was playing with him, and he knew it. Bad enough that he'd come all the way down only to find Slocum gone—most likely on the hunt for him— but now here he was, trapped inside this falling-down church with a bunch of women and an ugly punk.

On the other hand, he reminded himself, he had hostages.

That was some comfort.

But not much.

So where the hell was he? Without taking his gaze from the street, he said, "That woman. The one in the green dress. She from down here?"

The nun didn't answer, but Rome said, rather grandly, "Yeah, that's Mrs. Tanglewood. Me and my brother, we was hired to take her back home, to her rightful husband."

"And how'd you get mixed up with Slocum?"

The nun snapped, "Shut up!" before Rome could answer, and Joe pivoted again. Now, he hadn't mentioned Slocum's name up till this very minute, but it seemed like it had put everybody on edge.

The young nun, the one who was looking after the two

hurt ones, had turned to look at the one sitting beside Rome. And the one sitting beside Rome wasn't looking at Joe, but at Rome. And Rome looked like she was practically frying him with that stare.

A slow smile spread over Joe's face, because at that very moment, he *knew* that Slocum would be coming back. This time, it wasn't just a guess. It was sure and certain knowledge.

Silently, Slocum edged his way around the church. He didn't know who this bastard was, but he was going to meet his maker with Slocum's face imprinted on his brain.

He'd been crouching underneath the shuttered window long enough to know that somebody else had been hurt. He also knew where the sniper was—about a foot away, on the other side on a flimsy wood panel—but he couldn't tell about the others. Which put the kibosh on his initial feeling, which was to just send a rifle blast right through the shutters.

So he began to work his way around the church, hoping to find a window left ajar. After all, Beth had to have climbed out from somewhere, hadn't she? And the Sisters wouldn't have simply opened the door to the sniper.

He just hoped that somebody hadn't closed it up in the meantime.

The first window was locked up tight, and the second, and the third. But the shutters of the fourth, at the back corner of the building, were agape.

Slocum edged closer.

No light came through the opening.

Colt in hand, he slowly peered up, over the window's edge, then stood erect. It was clear. He quietly dropped his rifle to the cot inside, then soundlessly hoisted himself through the portal.

·19

Beth topped the hill and looked ahead, far into the distance. Were there lights? Yes. They were vague and hazy, but there were lights in this desert. Perhaps it was some kind of a dwelling, or maybe a cluster of buildings. It was hard to tell from such a distance.

She started walking down the hill, always keeping the distant lights in sight. Halfway down, she fell, and cursed herself when she saw what the tumble had done to her dress.

She spent the next few minutes shaking out her skirts like a disheveled Southern belle. And then she realized that the skirts weren't silk after all—they were plain dyed cotton, of all things!—and again wondered how on earth she had come to this horrible, desolate place.

And there was no one to save her, no one.

Well surely, if she just kept walking, someone would come to her aid. She'd go to the lights, and someone would help her. They would have to! She'd just tell them who she was, that was all.

And then she stopped again, for she realized that she had no idea who she was. She thought she must be important, but then, who would take an important lady and leave her in the middle of nowhere?

If only she could think, remember . . . *Concentrate,* she thought, *concentrate . . .*

She tumbled to the ground.

When she woke a few moments later, it was not as when she rose from sleep. It was the old familiar feeling of having lost time, and once again she knew who she was—Lizzie Conrad, the roughest, toughest lady cowpuncher and sharpshooter in the Wyoming Territory.

Except this didn't look much like Wyoming. But there, in the distance, was some sort of habitation. She saw a few lights burning, anyhow.

She gave a thoughtless hitch to her skirts and started marching toward the glow, thinking that dang, she should have brought her gun!

Slocum dropped softly down to the cot, retrieved his rifle, and crept toward the door. He was glad he wasn't wearing spurs. Panther didn't need them, and the jingle would have given him away.

He edged out into the narrow hall, and nearly stepped into a pool of congealing blood. If something had happened to Mother Grace . . .

There were no lights burning back here, but golden light fanned softly from the bend in the hall. Apparently, everybody was out front, in the church proper.

Which made sense. Whoever this man was, he'd want everybody where he could see them. And Mother Grace wasn't here, so that must mean she was alive. They were all alive, he hoped.

But when Slocum snuck a look out into the church, he realized that this man couldn't see any captives at all, because he was clear up by the front door, looking through a cracked shutter at the street outside.

Waiting.

Waiting for him.

He hadn't seen anybody else in the other rooms back

down the hall, so he assumed that the nuns and Rome were between him and their sniper. The sonofabitch even had his rifle's barrel resting on the windowsill. Pushed halfway through it, in fact.

Thought he was going to shoot ducks in a barrel, did he?

Under his breath, Slocum snorted. Fat chance of that.

After another quick look to make sure the sniper's sight was still trained upon the street, Slocum tiptoed up the hallway.

Mother Grace saw him first, and nearly gasped. But Slocum's finger, pressed to his lips, quieted her.

Rome, however, wasn't so smart. He opened his mouth in a great big grin and said, "Hey, Slocum!" before Mother Grace could elbow him in the ribs.

The man at the window moved faster than a heavyset man should have. He spun, leaving his rifle behind, caught in the window, and reached for his gun.

He barely cleared leather.

Slocum fired once, hitting him in the right shoulder, and the man cried out and dropped his weapon, crying, "You broke my arm, you sonofabitch!"

"Watch your language," Slocum snapped. "You're in a house of God."

Mother Grace had rushed forward almost immediately, and was retrieving the man's pistol from beneath a back pew, where it had landed. She said, "Sister Agnes?" and when the red-headed nun looked up, tossed it to her. Sister Agnes caught it quite handily, Slocum thought, and immediately trained it upon the intruder. Mother Grace then pulled the man's rifle from the window and aimed it down at him.

"What's your name?" Slocum demanded of the man.

Silence.

Slocum cocked his gun. "You already got me pretty riled, mister. You don't want to piss me off all the way."

"Why, I'm an old friend'a yours, Slocum," the fellow said.

The muscles in Slocum's jaw started to work, and Mother Grace—who must have been reading him like a book—quickly said, "Take this outside, gentlemen. Please. Otherwise, my finger might accidentally slip, and I'd be saying Hail Marys for the rest of my natural life."

"Aren't you going to patch me up, first?" asked the gunman with a lopsided grin. It didn't go all the way to his eyes, though. They were gray, and they were narrowed.

Slocum growled, "Move it."

Holding his wounded arm, their sniper started for the front door, and Slocum followed. If this bastard was an "old friend," he sure as hell didn't recognize him. Didn't much care to, either.

But by the time they'd gone out into the churchyard, his curiosity had gotten the better of him. He'd been planning just to march this idiot to the ramada, hog-tie him, and then haul him to Phoenix tomorrow. But now he asked, "All right, who are you?"

The man stopped walking and turned to face Slocum. "Been goin' by Fess Wilkerson lately. But you might remember me as Joe French."

Slocum remembered, and he found himself grinding his teeth. He said, "Thought you dropped off the map years ago."

"Yes and no," Joe replied. The bastard was still smirking behind that bushy white mustache of his.

"Figured you were scalped or froze to death," Slocum continued. "Guess fate ain't that kind."

Joe stopped smiling.

Slocum wiggled his gun and said, "Move. Over to the ramada."

Once he'd tied up Joe French and Sister Agnes came out with her rags and bowl of water—and, it turned out, a slim knife to dig the slug from Joe French's shoulder—Slocum asked Mother Grace to strip the tack off the horses and put them in the corral, then hiked up the street to find Panther. Beth's bay had already been wandering across the street when he marched Joe French outside.

So he caught the bay and led it back up to the little store with the goats penned behind it, and called, "Hello in there! Diego? It's Slocum!"

A moment later a window cracked open and the little Mexican man peeked out again. "Is it all right now, senor?" he asked warily. "The nuns, are they all right?"

Slocum said, "Everything's tidied up, amigo. You seen my horse? He's white with—"

"Black spots," said the man, nodding. "An Appaloosa. And I would be pleased if you would take him from my goat pen, Senor Slocum. My goats will stop giving milk if he keeps disturbing them."

Slocum, trying not to smile, said, "Be glad to, Diego."

The man disappeared and the shutter slammed shut, and Slocum, shaking his head in amusement, led the bay around to the back of the building. There, he found Panther, who had apparently jumped the fence. He was happily cutting a nanny goat from the herd all on his own, his reins swinging loose.

Needless to say, the goat looked pretty damned confused.

Slocum tied the bay, jumped the fence, and crossed to the horse. Panther had ceased his activity at Slocum's approach. He hung his head, as if he knew that this goat pen was someplace he wasn't supposed to be.

Slocum read his expression and muttered, "You're damn right, you old jughead," then rubbed the gelding's forehead. "C'mon, Panther," he said, leading the horse toward the fence. "We're getting out of here, fella. Gotta go and find that lunatic Beth. But this time, we're gonna use the gate."

Slocum shook his head as he led Panther from the corral. "Hoppin' fences to herd a bunch of damned goats. What's next? You gonna take up knitting?"

The moon was high and the stars were bright, and he ran into Beth about ten minutes' lope from town. Or rather, he ran afoul of her.

First, she ran from him, ran just like a tomboy, and hollered all sorts of unladylike things over her shoulder at him.

He was long past scratching his head over her antics, and bulldogged her like a calf—from horseback. He was tired, and he just wanted to get back to the church and get some shut-eye.

But Beth fought him, even after he'd shoved her to the ground.

"Leave me go, you hollow-tailed son of a range cow!" she shouted at one point.

He guessed this was a whole new side of her personality. He didn't have much time to dwell on it, though, because right after she screeched it into his ear, she kneed him in the crotch.

The word *pain* didn't have enough power to describe the sick feeling that shot through him, but he somehow managed to get her pinned. She was still struggling, but he held her there a minute while he gritted his teeth and tried to breathe.

When he could, he shouted, "Beth! Cut it out! It's me. Slocum."

Suddenly, she grew still.

In fact, she was so quiet that he thought she'd fainted. But her eyes were open, her lashes fluttering rapidly.

And then she said, "What do you think you're doing, you idiot! Get off me right now!"

Since the entire tone of her voice had changed, he did. Then he helped her up and watched her shake out her skirts.

"Good Lord!" she snarled. "What were you thinking, Slocum?"

"I might ask you the same damn thing, Beth," he replied, then turned to Panther, who had stopped nearby. "Fetch," he said, pointing to Beth's bay, who had kept on running for a bit, and had finally come to a halt a good hundred yards away.

Panther, always game, took off after him.

"What do you mean?" Beth asked.

Slocum sighed. "You know where you are?" He knew better, by now, than to ask if she knew who the hell she was.

She narrowed her eyes and glared at him. "Of course I do. I'm in Arizona. With you. And those filthy fools, Rome and London Granger." She looked around. "Well, I thought they were with us. Where'd they go?"

"London's dead and Rome's tied up back at the church."

"What church?"

Panther was pushing the bay toward them, Slocum noted. The horses couldn't get there quick enough for his taste.

"Beth, honey, it's a real long story."

20

Slocum settled down for the night outside the church, to keep watch on their two prisoners. Rome Granger had been moved outside. He slouched, slumped over and dozing, tied to the opposite side of the ramada, across from Joe French.

Joe French, too, appeared to be asleep. He'd been patched up by Sister Agnes, who reported that Joe's claims of a broken arm had been highly exaggerated. Slocum's slug, she said, as she took Beth inside, had passed nearly through the meat of his arm and hadn't even nicked the bone.

After he'd put Panther and the bay away for the night, he stretched out on his bedroll, which he'd placed across the ramada's absent front "wall," and only then did he remember that he hadn't eaten since noon.

It wasn't worth getting up, though. He was too tired to chew.

He didn't remember closing his eyes, but he must have, because when he woke up, dawn was just breaking, he had one hell of a headache, his holsters were empty, and Joe and Rome were gone.

So was Slocum's cash.

All ten thousand.

He stood up, hand to the aching goose egg on the back of his head, and swore so loudly and so continuously that he woke up Mother Grace and Sister Agnes, along with half the town.

Joe and Rome were a good seven miles from town by the time Slocum awoke.

It was Joe's favorite time of day, especially when he was moving to the west. He liked the sun at his back, liked the way his shadow loomed long, long, long, and narrow ahead of him.

He thought about mentioning this to Rome, then decided against it. Rome hadn't done much to inspire his trust, let alone his conversation.

In fact, he'd only brought Rome along to shut him up. Well, that, and because he'd managed to get himself untied, and then had been kind enough to untie Joe. Now Joe was wishing that he'd banged Rome over the head the same way he'd buffaloed Slocum.

Hell, the sonofabitch didn't even wake up!

But even though Rome had supposedly been busy saddling the horses, Joe had his suspicions that Rome had seen him going through Slocum's pockets. And he didn't know if Rome had any idea what Slocum had been carrying. Rome hadn't brought up the subject, and neither had Joe.

In fact, it was about to drive Joe crazy. It was pretty tough to enjoy the morning when you had to keep one eye on your saddle partner—if Rome could even be called that—the whole time.

Rome, whom Joe made sure was always riding along a little ahead of him, reined in his horse. Joe came to a halt, too. His shoulder was aching, but it didn't keep him from holding his hand at the ready, right near Slocum's gun.

That had given him a good bit of pleasure—taking Slocum's sidearms that was. Almost as much pleasure as finding the money, and realizing that it was all his, for true and real.

"Can we stop and grab some chuck?" Rome asked.

"Don't see why not," Joe answered amiably. Friendly Joe, that was him: Everybody's pal, everybody's neighbor, everybody's friend.

So long as it was to his advantage, that was.

Both men dismounted and watered their horses, who had been on the move through the night and seemed to appreciate the break. Then Rome opened his saddlebag and started rummaging around in it. Joe watched, eyes narrowed, just in case a pistol came out of there instead of food.

But only a possibles bag with a little jerky and a couple of apples appeared. Rome split it up, took a bite of his jerky, and said, "Hope we come to somethin' today. This takes care of the last of my stores."

Joe nodded. "Should get to Evenside by late afternoon. I'll shoot us a jackrabbit for noontime."

Rome said, "Better shoot two." His eyed his apple, and Joe knew why. They were awfully small. Rome continued, "This ain't much for a big feller like me. Or you, either."

Joe just kept on chewing. And thinking. Rome hadn't mentioned the money, but Joe was starting to think that he'd be better off with no witnesses after all—even possible witnesses. In fact, he didn't plan to go to Evenside at all. He planned to cut north, up into the hills, then do himself a whole lot of backtracking and brush-dragging to throw Slocum off his trail, just in case he'd survived that clubbing.

Of course, he didn't think that was hardly possible. He'd hit him twice.

Still, a man couldn't be too sure about anything.

He took a drink from his canteen and asked, "I never asked you, Rome. Why'd Slocum have you trussed up? Why was he takin' you in?"

Chewing, Rome said, "I don't know. I guess he was mad."

Joe cocked a brow.

"On account of me and my brother, London, trying to kill him and everything," Rome explained. He was intent on his food.

But Joe was still in the dark. He asked, "Why'd you try to kill him?"

"To get Mrs. Tanglewood back," Rome said around a mouthful of apple. "See, we tracked her down again and had her just about to home, when we sort of, um, borrowed Slocum's horse. 'Cept we should'a killed him all the way, because he tracked us down. Then later, when he took off with Mrs. Tanglewood and left us, we—"

"That's enough," Joe cut in. He'd followed the trail. He figured he could guess the rest. Not that it mattered very much. Old Rome was about to be dead, after all.

Well, Joe supposed he'd let Rome finish his breakfast first. A man deserved a last meal, didn't he?

Rome shrugged. "If you don't want to hear, I guess you don't want to hear."

"That's right," Joe answered, and turned to put his horse's nosebag away in his saddlebag.

Except that when he did, when the nosebag was halfway tucked inside, he heard an ominous *click* behind him.

Immediately, he stiffened. He whirled and reached for his gun, but his shoulder wound made him slower than usual, and Rome's weapon was already drawn.

Rome said flatly, "You killed my brother, you sono-fabitch."

The last thing to register on Joe French's brain was the sound of Rome's gun, blasting him into eternity.

Slocum mounted up, and Beth was at Panther's head.

"What am I supposed to do?" she demanded.

"Let go of Panther's bridle."

"But Slocum . . ."

"I mean it, damnit," he snapped.

Beth Tanglewood was the reason for all of this, from start to finish, he thought. He would have had a nice ride down to Phoenix and been in the arms of Rosie by now if it hadn't been for this crazy hellcat! How anybody could be so plumb loco and so beautiful at the same time was beyond him.

After what seemed like an age, Beth finally let go of Panther's bridle and took a step back.

"You're going to leave me here with these nuns," she said accusingly. "You're going to ride off and I'll never see you again."

Slocum sighed. He wanted to get out of here, and fast. But he said, "Don't you think that'd be for the best, Beth?"

"Whose best?" she suddenly snarled, her face changing, suddenly older, twisted, tired, and more demanding than pleading. "Just who would it be better for, you bastard?"

"I give up," he said, and reined Panther away from her. "Go back in with the sisters," he called as he rode out of the yard, following the trail left by Rome Granger and his "old pal" Joe French.

He heard her shout, "Screw you, you pissant peckerwood!" but he didn't look back.

He pushed Panther into a lope and sped across the desert, headed after Rome and Joe.

Rome stood there for a few moments, staring at the body. He'd hit Joe French directly in the heart, judging by the amount of blood that suddenly welled from his chest—and then stopped. And Joe hadn't even gotten off a shot at him.

"There you go, London," he whispered. "You're revenged, by God."

And then he spat on Joe's body. He gave it a couple of kicks, too, just to make sure.

He didn't want to make any mistakes, like he'd done with Slocum.

If only they'd taken a few seconds to bash in his skull with a rock! It wasn't like there weren't any around. Hell, the whole place had been practically all rock.

But no, he and London were in a hurry. They wanted to hustle Mrs. Tanglewood back to that wife beater as fast as they could. He reckoned that he'd beat her, too, if she tried that on him. Changing all the time, that was. If he'd been married to her, he wouldn't have put up with that shit at all.

He heaved a sigh, then walked around Joe's corpse to the gray horse. The gelding must sure be trained good, that was all he could figure. It hadn't hardly moved at all when he fired his gun.

He supposed that Joe must have fired his gun or rifle a whole lot around that horse, for him to stand so quiet like that. It made Rome feel kind of justified, as if he had done the greater society a favor.

Hell, they ought to be downright grateful to him!

At least, he hoped that London, wherever he was, had gotten some good from it. Imagine, a man killing your brother, spending half the night with you in a shed with his body, then riding off with you! Didn't Joe French have any sense?

He began to unfasten the girth on Joe's gray. Well, in retrospect, he guessed Joe did have some sense, after all. He'd made Rome ride in the lead the whole time. Joe was probably watching him, Rome thought, watching to see if he was going to make a move.

"Hell," he said as he pulled the gray's saddle off and set it on the gravelly ground. "I'll bet you anything that if I hadn't killed that bastard, he was fixin' to kill me!"

The gray chose that moment to bob his head, and Rome said, "See? I was right!"

Having been more than vindicated by Joe's own horse—it was a sign, he told himself—Rome stripped off the gelding's bridle, then slapped him on the rump.

The horse just stood there.

"Go on! You're free till somebody else catches you," he said, then whooped and flapped his arms.

The gelding took one last long look at him, then Joe, then hit a gallop inside two strides, leaving nothing behind but his dust.

"That's better," Rome muttered.

He went to Joe's saddlebags, and did, indeed, find a vittles bag. This he took, along with the canteens that had been hanging from Joe's saddle horn.

He never touched the body. Not once, except for those first two kicks. He figured that Joe wasn't worth it.

He mounted his horse, reined it north, and took off at a jog. He'd been thinking, and he guessed that Canada was his best bet for escaping the wrath of Bass Tanglewood. Of course, Mexico was a lot closer, but he was sick of the heat—and it was hotter down there—and he didn't speak Spanish. He didn't have much affinity for languages.

Someplace where they talked American was more to his liking.

Well, maybe up there they called it talking "Canadian."

Didn't much matter, did it?

And besides, he'd heard that there was someplace on the far west coast of Canada that was just like the tropics, only gentler. Something about the ocean currents keeping it from freezing like the rest of the country.

There were palm trees there, a mild climate, the whole shebang. Maybe pretty girls, too.

Paradise.

A half-sad smile spreading over his lips, he pushed the horse into a lope.

21

At about ten in the morning, Slocum rode up on Joe French's body. Quickly, he took in the scene. There was Joe's tack, stripped from his horse, with a single line of prints—undoubtedly Rome's—heading off to the north and another single line, left by a horse that wasn't carrying anybody or anything. Joe had been shot clean through the heart.

Slocum dismounted and sighed. At least Rome had had the presence of mind to strip Joe's mount before he set it free. The horse was nowhere in sight.

After he made sure the Joe was dead, he went to the man's saddlebags, but found nothing there except the usual trail equipment. He supposed that Rome had made off with Joe's water and food. But there was no cash in them, none at all.

Next, he rolled out the bedroll to make certain nothing was hidden in it. There wasn't.

Lastly, he searched the body.

This was far more fruitful. He found his own ten thousand, divvied into the same three wads of cash that he'd been carrying it in, and an extra fifteen dollars, which he also pocketed, muttering, "Burial fee," at the corpse.

He took his guns back from Joe, but he couldn't find his little pocket derringer or Rome's gun, which he'd been carrying in his belt. He supposed those had gone off north, with Rome.

He pulled down his collapsible shovel from his pack, locked it into place, and began to look for the softest place to dig.

When he was finished, having carried scores of rocks to make a cairn over the shallow grave—but not having planted a cross—he sat down in Panther's shade and rolled himself a quirlie. Joe's bedroll had gone to cover the body before he started shoveling the gravelly dirt back in the hole, but he'd left the saddle and bridle out, carefully covering the saddle with its blanket. Maybe somebody'd come along who could use it.

He stared to the north, at Rome's track. He could follow it. He should, really.

But burying Joe had reminded him that there was still London's corpse to attend to, back at the Sisters of Mercy in Santa Rosa.

And besides, Rome was, if not much else, a great tracker. He'd find a way to muddle his trail once he got out of this desert, and frankly, Slocum didn't want to think about wasting his time trying to uncover it.

No, he'd let Rome go and find his own end. Whether that would be at the hands of Bass Tanglewood or a long life spent in Australia or somewhere else was up to Rome. And fate.

He finished his smoke, checked Panther's girth, remounted, and headed back toward the church at a slow jog.

"She wouldn't want to go back the way she came," Bass Tanglewood said. He stood on the porch with Donner, whose horse was saddled, provisioned, and waiting at the bottom of the steps for his rider.

"So any way but north," Donner said, flatly.

"Correct," replied Tanglewood. "Try Phoenix first. It's a decent-sized hamlet. She could take a train or a stage from there. Check both depots, all the hotels, all the—"

"I know," said Donner, pulling on a glove impatiently.

"Yes," Tanglewood said. "I suppose you do." He dug into his pocket and pulled out a small roll of bills. "Take the train as far as you can. And hurry. And if you run across Rome and London? Take care of them."

Donner said nothing, only nodded curtly, then went down the steps to his horse.

He swung up on it, and reined it away from the rail.

"And wire me," Tanglewood called as Donner rode out of sight. "Twice a day, when you can!"

Donner didn't turn around. He simply doffed his hat for a moment, then rode on.

Tanglewood waited until Donner was out of sight before he went into the house.

Slowly, he mounted the main stairway and climbed to the top, pausing briefly on the landing to check one last time for Donner. All he saw was a small cloud of dust on the eastern horizon.

He continued on to the second floor, walked to the end of the hall, and pulled a small ring of keys from his back pocket. One of these, he used to open the last door.

He stepped inside, went to the chair, and sat down.

A person never would have known the things that had happened in here, he thought. The coverlet and canopy were bleached muslin, stark white, as were the white eyelet pillow shams. There was no blood in evidence.

Everything, in fact, was painted white or gilded gold or both, much in the style of the French, and completely spotless. It suited her. And it suited his tastes, too, to beat her in the midst of so much opulence, to tatter her flesh and ruin the drapes and bed linens with streaks and spatters of her blood.

They had a constant supply of fresh things that took up an entire chifforobe.

A person wouldn't have known anything by the stores of whips and flails and paddles and gags and harnesses, either. Those were all safely locked away in the French-style "hope chest" at the foot of her bed.

Again, he had to grin at that. The logic of it seemed so . . . circular.

Mother Grace happened to be outside when Slocum first appeared on the horizon. She had mixed feelings about the fact that he was back so soon, and that he was alone. She genuflected, said a brief prayer for the souls—lost or not— of Joe and Rome, and dipped her bucket in the well. It would be a few minutes until he came into hailing distance, anyway. Best to get the water that Sister Agnes had requested.

Sisters Dominique and Naomi were on the mend. Sister Agnes had said that Sister Dominique had actually sat up this morning and insisted on going to the altar for her morning prayers, but Sister Agnes had vetoed that notion. Mother Grace agreed.

Naomi was awake and fairly bright, but winced at every movement. Sister Agnes was taking pains to see that her wound remained constantly clean.

She was, in fact, cleaning it again—the reason she'd need more water.

Mother Grace poured some from her bucket into Sister Agnes's enamel bowl, then proceeded on to what passed for their kitchen. An iron sink, which drained to the outside vegetable patch, a table and chairs, a few curtained cupboards, a larder chest filled with foodstuffs they'd canned from the gardens of past years, and a battered wood-burning stove. She set the bucket on the table, then went back outside to wait for Slocum.

He was still a good way off, but she lifted a hand to him, and he waved back. At least, while she waited, she could collect the eggs. She should have done it long ago, but there was so much to tend to this morning.

By the time she'd wrested today's eggs from the hens and thrown down some chicken feed for them, Slocum pulled the saddle off that Appaloosa of his and turned it loose in the corral.

"Good morning," she said as she walked up to him, the egg basket over her arm.

"Wipe that expression off your face," was the first thing he said to her. She hadn't realized she had any expression, but perhaps that was what he meant. "I didn't kill anybody," he explained. "Buried somebody, though."

When Sister Grace's face twisted into an unspoken question, he said, "Joe French. Seems that Rome did it. Probably revenge for that."

He pointed to the ramada, where London's body still lay under a blanket, tucked back into a corner. Flies were beginning to buzz at the blanket's edges.

"Can't say that I blame him too much," he said. "You got a shovel around here? I hate usin' that little one I carry with me."

Mother Grace pointed him toward the shovel, showed him the little graveyard behind the church, then left him. Sister Dominique usually did the cooking, but it was up to her, now.

And it was almost time for lunch.

When Slocum had finished digging the hole—which took him three hours, though he was able to dig it deeper than he had Joe French's final resting place—he went in the church to cool off and get another drink of water.

He found no one in the main chapel, and went up to the front, and down the hall. Immediately, he smelled something that made his stomach begin to rumble and his saliva begin to work overtime.

"In here, Slocum," called Mother Grace, and he followed her voice into the little kitchen. There, he found her filling a plate with beef stew and biscuits.

"No arguments," she said as she slid it onto the table between neatly set out silverware.

He pulled out the chair. "You won't get any from me," he replied, smiling, and picked up his fork.

Mother Grace stopped him. "Father," she said, her head bowed, "for what this man is about to receive, he is truly grateful. He just won't say so. Amen."

Slocum chuckled and dug in. It was mighty fine grub.

When he'd finished that—and then a second helping, while telling her all about his morning—she pulled out a peach pie and cut him a wide wedge, which he practically inhaled.

Then he sat back, rubbing his stomach, and said, "You still cook like an angel, Mother Grace."

"Thank you," she said. She was sitting across from him. "Some things, one never forgets." She shook her head. "That nice Mr. Granger. I mean, comparatively speaking. I would never have guessed it of him."

"He tried to kill me, you know," Slocum cut in.

Mother Grace nodded. "Yes, true. But he didn't succeed, did he?"

Slocum chuckled. "All right. You win. You've already said about the Sisters. How's Beth doing?"

Mother Grace said, "She is a very sad woman," and shook her head slowly. "Have you seen her back?"

"Yeah." And when Mother Grace shot him a look, he quickly added, "Just briefly."

"It was enough to tell you all you needed to know, then?" she asked.

"That, and a whole lot more." Slocum poured himself a fresh cup of coffee. "But how's she doin'? In her head, I mean?"

Mother Grace shrugged. "It's difficult to tell. She was very agitated after you rode out."

"I'll bet."

"Sister Agnes gave her something to calm her. She's sleeping now."

Slocum nodded. "Good. She didn't get much sleep last night."

"Neither did you," Mother Grace said with a smile.

Slocum snorted. "Yeah, but I'm used to keepin' doctors' hours."

Mother Grace's smile broadened into a grin. "Go ahead. I know you're dying to."

"What?"

"Smoke."

He had been wanting a quirlie. He reached for his pouch but paused. "You sure?"

"When the priest comes every other month, he smokes," she said. "In fact, he keeps tobacco here. I'm certain he wouldn't mind if you—"

Slocum waved off the idea. "That's fine Grace. I like my own just fine. I ain't sank so low that I need to rob a priest's tobacco pouch."

Mother Grace nodded, and smiled as she watched him roll, then light the quirlie. "Just like when I was home with Papa."

"That was a long time ago."

"Not so long. You must remember, Slocum, you were fresh from the War Between the States when you first came to Mexico and met Papa. I was only ten, then. I remember how you used to sit at the table for hours, smoking and drinking and talking about grown-up things."

Slocum grinned, and exhaled a plume of smoke through his nostrils. "You were supposed to be asleep, you little monkey." And then he thought better of what he'd said. "'Scuse me, Mother."

She laughed, just like a girl.

22

After a small ceremony with the nuns, who had already marked a cross for the grave, Slocum pulled Mother Grace aside and slipped her one thousand and fifteen dollars. The thousand was from him, and the fifteen, he figured was from Joe French's "estate."

"To fix your shutters, and whatever else needs it," he said when she started to protest.

Slocum rode out. He left Beth behind. She was still sleeping, and besides, he doubted that she'd recall that last conversation they'd had, anyhow.

It only took him a half hour to ride into Phoenix, a little town that, up until a few years ago, had been called Pumpkinville. The city fathers had changed its name to reflect the great things they hoped were coming, and also to reflect its past. The valley in which it rested had once been the center of a long-vanished Indian civilization, which left behind only its ball courts, a few dwellings, and a series of irrigation canals, which were once again in use today.

The town had grown some since the last time Slocum was here, which hadn't been that long ago. There were four new houses, one under construction, on the road Slocum chose to ride in on, and there was a new saloon going up on Washington Street.

Farther down Washington Street was Slocum's goal: Stella's Place, and Rosie. Ah, the delightful Rosie, with her sunny smile and twinkling eyes and buxom figure!

He rode up to the rail, dismounted, and looped Panther's reins over it. Rubbing his hands together in anticipation, he entered Stella's Place.

"Slocum!" Stella bellowed when she saw him. He caught her up in his arms and she gave him a big smooch on the cheek. "My God!" she said after he let her down. "It's been a coon's age!"

He laughed. "Only six months, Stella. Rosie still workin' for you?"

Stella grinned. "As if she'd work anyplace else! She's out doin' some marketing with a couple of the gals, Slocum, but if'n you wanna wait, she won't be—"

Slocum silenced her with a wave of his hand. "Nah, I've got some business to take care of first." He dug into his pocket and pulled out the money clip, which was the smallest roll of bills he had. It was still mighty impressive, though.

He peeled off several bills and handed them to Stella, who looked at them, then up at Slocum. She appeared stupefied by shock, and Slocum held back a chuckle.

"If it's all right with you and with her, I'd like to buy all of Rosie's time for the next few days," he said.

Stella's shock quickly changed back to warm hospitality. She jammed the bills down the front of her dress and said, "You gonna be stayin' here?"

"If you don't mind, Stella."

She grinned. "That's just fine and dandy by me, Slocum. Now, you go get your things, and I'll have 'em took up to Rosie's room."

Slocum tipped his hat, then went back outside for his saddlebags and bedroll.

After delivering them into the hands of a giggling parlor girl, he rode up the street, and to the sheriff's office.

Now, Slocum'd had an uneasy relationship with Sheriff Bob Treadwell ever since that little disagreement over a reward—privately offered—for the MacNally gang. He hoped that Treadwell had decided to let bygones be bygones, or he was liable to end up wasting a whole lot of time in the sheriff's office explaining and re-explaining himself. He'd seen Treadwell at work.

But the sheriff greeted him, if not with a great big grin, with at least a sort of smile. A good sign, Slocum figured, because he knew that Treadwell couldn't lie to save his life.

"How you doin', you old peckerwood?" Treadwell said, slapping him on the shoulder. "Come on in! Got a pot of coffee brewin'!"

Slocum had a cup, and then a second, and while the men drank coffee and smoked, Slocum explained about Beth and the Granger boys and Joe French. He didn't leave a blessed thing out, either.

Sheriff Treadwell puffed on his pipe silently for a few moments after Slocum finished. And then he said, "That's quite a tale. In fact, if anybody but you had come in here and spun me that yarn, I wouldn't have believed him. 'Course, I'm not entirely sure I believe you."

Slocum was about to open his mouth with a protest when Treadwell's lips quirked into a grin.

"Gotcha," he said.

"Cockeyed bastard," said Slocum, and slouched back into his chair.

Treadwell laughed. "You deserved it. I don't think I have to say why."

Treadwell didn't. But still, Slocum had agreed to split the reward on the MacNally gang with him. Seemed to him that he hadn't entirely merited that little trick.

"I've heard of Bass Tanglewood," Treadwell continued. "Powerful man, and not an awful nice one, from what I've heard. You can bet your boots that he's gonna be sending somebody after the three of them."

"I figured."

"Probably be sending them here, too," Treadwell said with some degree of resignation. "Thanks a whole helluva lot, Slocum."

It was Slocum's turn to grin. "No problem, Bob. Glad to be of service."

"Sonofabitch."

"Bastard."

"At least I'm a self-made man," Treadwell retorted.

Slocum grinned at him, then stood up. "Just thought I'd let you know," he said. "I'll be up at Miss Stella's, if you need me for anything."

Treadwell cocked a brow. "Rosie?"

"Who else?"

Rosie's room was smallish, but papered in rose wallpaper with little violets, cozy, and most important, it had a big, soft bed next to the window. There was also a rocking chair beside the door, and this was where Slocum waited.

He'd already put Panther up at the livery, stopped by the bank to secure most of his money, picked up a couple bottles of champagne and a box of cigars for himself, and for Rosie, a couple of pounds of fancy chocolates and a big bouquet of flowers. He was all set.

Now, all he needed was the girl herself.

He had almost dozed off in the rocker when he heard the door open. In walked Rosie, all dark hair and lush figure.

She didn't see him at first. All she saw was the bounty he'd placed on her bed. Then she whirled around, crying, "Slocum?" and practically threw herself into his arms. He didn't have time to stand up, and the back of the rocker hit the wall with a *thump!*

He didn't much notice it, though. He was busy with Rosie's lips.

They were just as delicious as he remembered, shaped like rosebuds, and her skin was just as creamy and smooth. She wore little makeup, as opposed to the other girls. Her beauty was natural. She pulled back a little, and batting dark, long-lashed eyes, said, "Oh, Slocum! How long can you stay?"

"Long as you like," he murmured. "I'm all yours, baby."

"Mmm," she hummed happily. "Let's get started, then."

She rose, and put a hand down to him. Eagerly, he stood, too, and began to unbutton his shirt.

She worked at the buttons on her dress, saying, "It's been a long time since you been through, baby."

"Six months," he said, peeling out of his shirt. He unfastened his belt buckle.

"That's about five months and four weeks too long," she said, shimmying out of her dress. It dropped into a pool about her ankles, and she began untying her petticoats.

He stopped unbuttoning his britches long enough to snort out a laugh.

She looked down and arched a pretty brow. "Your boots, Slocum?"

Feigning abashment, he sat down in the rocking chair again, his britches at half mast, and stuck out one booted foot. She took it between her legs with her petticoated backside to him. He placed the other booted foot on her rear end and pushed while she pulled.

The boot came off, and they repeated the process. God, she had a sweet fanny! He couldn't wait until she got out of those petticoats.

She shucked them—and her camisole—while he got free of the rest of his clothes, and he swept her up in his arms, kissing first her lips, then the crown of each breast.

He carried her to the bed, then playfully dropped her onto it before falling atop her. Giggling, she caught him in her arms, then hugged him close.

"I missed you so much, Slocum," she whispered, as she moved aside the box of candy.

He slid the bottle of champagne to the floor. "Been thinking about you for the last hundred miles, Rosie," he said.

She parted her legs and brought them up to hug his thighs. "Then let's not waste any more time, baby," she murmured.

He didn't.

He eased into her slowly, enjoying the drawn-out hiss she made when he did so. And then he began to move, slowly at first, gradually gathering speed.

She moved with him, matching him stroke for stroke, and he pushed himself up on his elbows so that he could watch those round, firm breasts shiver with every powerful thrust, see her eyes half-lidded, her lips pursing, and the fine skin of sweat that was emerging on her brow.

She was a pip, his Rosie. Well, his until the money ran out, that was.

All too soon, he felt the itch between his legs begin to escalate into a fire, and he began to move faster, thrusting, then pounding into her.

She, too, must have felt her own fire building, because she arched her back and started making little noises, urging him on, urging him to move faster, harder. Her nails raked his back, and he felt himself about to explode.

And when he felt her gathering, gathering beneath him toward her own climax, he gave three more dynamic thrusts, and felt her writhe in a teeth-jarring climax— which brought him to his own fruition. Three more strokes to finish it for both of them, and then he rolled to the side.

Right on top of the candy box.

He pulled it out from beneath his back and tossed it to the foot of the bed.

Rosie was panting, but she managed a laugh. And then she rolled toward him, onto her side, and hugged his chest. "I do so like you, Slocum."

He chuckled and hugged her back, then kissed her temple, whispering, "Me, too, Rosie. Me too."

Donner loaded his horse onto the Colorado River ferry and tied it to the hitching post before he moved over to the observation rail.

The Colorado was just as muddy as he remembered, and just as wide. Dirty old river, he thought.

He'd made excellent time down from Tanglewood's place. He planned to make good time to Phoenix, as well. Of course, Tanglewood had to be wired every damn five minutes. That took a toll on his time. What did Tanglewood think? That there was a telegrapher's office every five miles in the middle of the Arizona desert?

Apparently, he thought with a grimace.

Well, he'd wire once from Yuma, but after that, who knew?

He didn't much like his boss, but he was the best paying employer for a long way in any direction. And he supposed that whether a man liked or disliked the fellow he worked for didn't matter a whit in this world. The money was what was important, and Donner was building up quite a stash.

The other men laughed at him—behind his back, of course, for they knew it was dangerous to laugh at him to his face—because he never blew his pay on whiskey or beer or women, never bought anything more than a bag of horehound candy every once in a while, or those long, black cigarettes he favored, or the occasional new shirt.

But he knew better. While they were drinking and pissing away their wages, he had his eye on a piece of land.

He'd already put the down payment on it, as a matter of fact.

It would be a good place to retire to when he got too old to handle a gun with the precision required by his current trade. The place had woods and a crystal clear creek, and plenty of game. Four hundred acres of it. He had no plans to farm. Farming was for idiots.

No, he could just live off the land, and live quite happily.

He preferred venison to beef, anyhow, and rabbit and wild ducks and quail to chicken. He liked shooting them better than people, too. Leastwise, they didn't shoot back at you.

Vegetables and feed and other things, he could buy in town. There was one, just the beginnings of a little place called Silver Springs City, about five or six miles from his place.

His place. He liked the sound of it.

He'd already snuck up there once or twice, and he had a cabin staked out: just wood and twine for walls, but a cabin, nonetheless. It wasn't too big or too small, but just right for a single man who wanted to live comfortably and quietly, with just his rifle and some books for company.

And by the time he got too over-the-hill to earn his living with his Colt, the house would be finished or close to it, and he wouldn't feel too much like baling hay and shucking corn, anyhow.

No. No farming for him.

The ferry docked at the Arizona side with a thump, and he unhitched his horse from the post.

Giving a curt nod to the captain, he disembarked, then tightened his mount's girth again. He'd loosened it for the boat trip.

He mounted up and set off toward the east, first to Yuma to send Tanglewood his damned telegram, and then toward Phoenix.

23

"Do you know where you are, my dear?" Mother Grace asked.

"Of course," replied Beth. "I'm in some church in the backwater of nowhere, except there isn't any water because this is the Arizona Territory."

Mother Grace smiled. "Do you know who brought you here?"

"That sonofabitch, Slocum," Beth replied curtly, then blushed and seemed to think better of it. "Sorry, Mother."

Mother Grace patted her hand. "I'll have Sister Agnes bring you some tea. Or would you rather get up and come sit in the kitchen?"

Beth said, "You know there's going to be trouble, don't you?"

"I think there's already been a great deal of trouble, my dear."

"There'll be more," Beth said cryptically, and stared away, out the window. "He'll send Donner next."

"Donner? Who's Donner?"

Beth turned back toward her, suddenly beaming like a child. "Do you have cake to go with that tea? And I'd rather have milk, please, ma'am."

•   •   •

In Phoenix, Slocum and Rosie were having a late supper down the street at the Bluebird Café. Rosie had ordered the fried chicken dinner, and Slocum dug into his steak. The morning marathon had built up quite an appetite in both of them, he thought.

Five times! That had to be close to a record, even for him!

Rosie looked up from her plate. "You said that both these Granger brothers are out of the picture. But Tanglewood's a powerful man. I mean, even *I've* heard of him! Don't you think it's possible that he'll send someone else? After all, she is his wife."

Slocum swallowed a mouthful of beef. "But not his property."

Rosie shook her head sadly. "She's chattel, Slocum. That's just the way of the world. Why do you think I'm doing what I do?"

He'd never thought to ask, but he was suddenly curious. After all, she was smart and she was beautiful. She could have had her pick of men.

So he asked, "Why?"

"Because I won't be owned by any man," she said, then matter-of-factly added, "No offense intended, Slocum."

"None taken."

She smiled. "See, I make good money. A helluva lot more than I'd make if I were a schoolmarm. Or a store clerk. Or if I washed dishes or was a seamstress. That's about all there is for women who don't wish to marry. I'm savin' my money, Slocum."

She leaned closer and whispered, "I been working on my back for over ten years, now, and I've got a little over fifteen thousand dollars saved up in one bank or another. Can't trust it all to one place, since they tend to get robbed. I'd have closer to eighteen grand if some sonofabitch hadn't robbed the Quartzite bank a couple years ago. . . ."

Slocum's brows shot up. "Good Lord, Rosie! That's a whole lot of money!"

She smiled smugly. "Don't I know it. When I get to twenty grand, that's when I retire. I'm going to move to San Francisco, change my name, and be a real lady. Maybe a widow, I haven't decided yet."

Suddenly, Slocum knew where part of his remaining nine thousand was going to go. He wanted her to have it, to go to the big city and live that kind of life.

Of course, maybe she'd be grateful enough that if and when he went to Frisco, she'd "remember" him fondly. . . .

But all he said was, "I think that's a damned good plan, Rosie."

She nodded. "Me, too." Then, twisting in her chair, she shouted over her shoulder, "Hey, Sam! Can we get some more coffee over here?"

By almost midnight, a very tired Donner rode into Phoenix. He was falling asleep in the saddle, and his horse was exhausted. He'd kept up quite a pace.

So he roused the man at Flynn's Livery, paid him extra to settle his horse at such a late hour, and went straight to the hotel.

He figured that by morning, he could ask around town. Of maybe he'd throw caution to the wind and go see the sheriff. They usually knew what was going on in their towns. Of course, he couldn't go as himself. He'd go as Dennis, Wayne Dennis, a name he used often, and make his inquiries.

And Tanglewood could damn well wait until morning to get his stupid wire.

He fell asleep almost immediately, his Colt tucked beneath his pillow and his hand mere inches from it. Old habits died hard.

He slept through until nearly nine in the morning.

•   •   •

Slocum woke with his arms around Rosie. It was a good feeling. Drowsing, she cuddled against him, a soft smile curling her lips. Gently, he stroked her creamy skin from nape to butt, and her eyes softly fluttered open.

"Good morning," she purred.

"Mornin'," he replied. He toyed with the silken strands at her temple.

"I wish you could stay forever," she whispered, and then seemed to think better of it. "I mean, I don't want you to . . . Oh, hell. You know what I mean."

Slocum chuckled. "Don't worry, Rosie. You ain't in no danger of taking me on as a husband."

She closed her eyes. "You do understand, then. Slocum, what would I do without you?"

"Probably very well."

She opened one eye and hoisted a brow. "Riddles. Why do you always have to talk in riddles?"

"Oh, I don't always."

"Well, sometimes you do."

Again, he chuckled. He reached over her and turned the bedside clock to face him. "Ten-thirty," he said. "I guess we outdid ourselves after we got back from dinner."

"You're not just whistlin' Dixie," she said with a grin. "I swear, Slocum, you're the most man in one package on the face of this earth. And no, don't ask me to go again. I gotta find out if I can still walk, first."

He laughed.

She slid out of bed, still naked, and took a few tentative steps. "So far, so good," she said, and pulled on a robe. Letting herself out the door, she said, "Be right back, darlin'."

He knew she was going to the outhouse, but his bladder was suddenly feeling too urgent to make the trek down the steps and outside. He went to the side window—which fortunately faced the alley—opened it and checked to make sure it was empty, and then took a long and very satisfying piss out the window.

Life was good.

That was, until somebody banged on the door with his fist, and then Sheriff Bob Treadwell shouted, "Slocum! Slocum, you in there?"

He was starting to pound some more when Slocum snatched a sheet off the bed, wrapped it around his middle, while calling, "I'm here, damnit Bob! Come on in!"

Treadwell nearly fell into the room, for he was in such a hurry that he tripped over his own feet. Slocum caught him by an elbow and kept him from going all the way down.

"Thanks," Bob said.

"Welcome," said Slocum. "What the hell is goin' on to get you so riled up?"

Treadwell collapsed in the rocker and hung his head. "I loused it up, Slocum. I think I loused it up pretty damned good."

Slocum sat down on the edge of the bed. "What you talkin' about, Bob?"

"Wayne Dennis."

"Wayne Dennis who?"

"That was what he told me," Treadwell said, his head still downcast. "He said he was her brother. Aw, hell. You know I can't lie worth a damn, Slocum."

Slocum shook his head. "Whose brother? You wanna back up about a quarter mile?"

Fifteen minutes later, Slocum was striding down Washington Street toward the livery. Damn that Bob Treadwell, anyhow! He hadn't even had a chance to say good-bye to Rosie.

Treadwell had loused things up good, all right. All this Wayne Dennis character—and Slocum was pretty damned sure his name was Donner—had to do was ask, and Treadwell had blabbed out the whole thing—London was dead, Rome was gone, and Beth was in hiding at the Sisters of Mercy. Hell, he'd even given Donner directions!

With friends like that, who needed enemies?

Which was why, as a parting gesture, Slocum had slugged the sheriff in the jaw.

At least he'd had a chance to tell Stella that he'd be back, and that Rosie shouldn't worry. Except, he thought as he quickly saddled Panther, maybe it couldn't hurt if she worried just a little. After he'd woken up to the fact that it was Donner, that was.

He didn't figure Donner was a man to be taken lightly.

And Donner had at least an hour's head start on him. He'd have to ride like hell to catch up with him.

And that was exactly what he did. He moved Panther rapidly toward that dusty little town, pacing him carefully, slowing to a jog, then gearing back up into a full-blown gallop.

Panther was one tough horse. Slocum just thanked his lucky stars that they didn't pass a herd of cattle or pronghorn on the way north. That would have been the last thing he needed.

When at last he reached Santa Rosa and the Sisters of Mercy, he circled the town first, and rode in from the north. You couldn't be too careful.

And as it turned out, he was right. The streets were as empty as when they'd fought it out with Joe French.

He reined in along the same little building with the goats behind it, figuring that they'd keep Panther busy for a while, and crept forward, gun drawn.

There was a new horse tied to the ramada, and alongside it stood Beth's bay, saddled and ready.

"Shit," Slocum hissed through clenched teeth. "Here we go again."

24

Before Slocum could cross the street—or even think about cutting back around, behind the church—the front doors banged open.

There was the man Slocum assumed was Donner, and he was pulling Beth, kicking and screaming, by her wrist. Beth was quickly followed by Mother Grace, who pleaded with Donner not to take her, that she was sick, and didn't he realize how badly she'd been treated?

But Donner paid her no heed, other than to threaten to backhand her. When Mother Grace didn't back off at that, he pulled his side arm and aimed it at her. At this, she faltered a little and genuflected, but she stood her ground.

In the meantime, Slocum drew his Colt and leveled it at Donner. If only Beth would stop moving around so much! She was struggling, practically dancing between him and his target, and every time he thought he might be able to get off a shot, she moved between them again.

At last, Donner forced her up on her horse and tied her hands to the saddle horn, but he was sheltered by his horse's body as he did so. Then, he finally moved out into the open to get on his own horse.

Slocum fired.

The slug missed, for at the last second Donner wheeled about to slap Beth, who had just called him a cocksucker. Slocum didn't know who she was this time, but she surely had a foul mouth, and he grinned.

But only momentarily.

Donner ducked back inside the ramada, Mother Grace fled back to the church, and the horses scattered. Beth was on the back of the bay, with absolutely no way to control it. And Panther, who normally would have barreled after her, was busy herding the damned goats!

First things first.

Slocum was just about to take another shot, when Donner's slug splintered the wood beside his face, piercing it with splinters. It stung like hell, but it was no worse than Mother Grace had gotten.

Blood running down his face, Slocum quickly backed up and skirted the rear of the building, muttering, "Knothead" as he passed Panther and the goats.

He came up the other side of it, swiftly crossing over to the next building before he edged toward the street. He peered around the building's corner.

Donner was gone.

Great. This was going to be more work than Slocum had planned on.

He inched a little farther forward and looked up and down the little street. It wasn't like Donner had a whole raft of hiding places to choose from in Santa Rosa.

And then Slocum had a thought. What if Donner had figured out what he was doing? What if he was planning on coming up from behind?

He crept back, retracing his steps and crossing the narrow alley as quietly as he could. He peered around the back of the building, into the goat pen that he'd just crossed.

Sure enough, there was Donner. And he took a shot at Slocum, who ducked back. The sonofabitch thought fast on his feet, that was for sure! Slocum thought as he quickly dropped to squat on his heels.

He returned fire, but Donner didn't see him. Despite being hit in the arm, Donner fired again at exactly the same time as Slocum, but at the place where Slocum had been standing.

Slocum got him in the arm, but there had to be an end to this.

Grimacing, Slocum pulled the trigger again. This time, he had a better chance to aim, and Donner fell to his knees, shot through the forehead. His blood spurted out over the closest goat's back before he fell all the way down, face in the dirt.

His gun still aimed at Donner, Slocum slid through the fence and checked the body.

Dead.

Then he whistled for Panther—who, for the moment, had stopped herding to listen to the gunfire—and led him from the goat pen, before dragging out Donner's body. Latching the gate behind him, he first led Panther out into the street and pointed him toward Beth's horse, which had come to a halt about a hundred and fifty yards out.

"Fetch," he said, and as the horse happily cantered off, he said, "Do something useful for a change."

Then he went back for Donner. But the time he'd dragged him into the street, a little knot of people had gathered, Mother Grace among them.

She crossed herself, said a silent prayer, then looked up. "It was necessary, I suppose?" she asked.

"Either him or me."

"Come," she said. "Let Sister Agnes see to your face."

He'd forgotten that he was bleeding.

Panther was back with Beth by the time they reached the church, and Slocum waved off Mother Grace while he untied Beth's hands and helped her down. For the moment,

she was mute and appeared totally bewildered, as if she
had no idea what had just happened to her.

It was just as well. After having run out on Rosie, barreled up here full speed, and nearly gotten his head shot
off, the last thing he needed was to fight her all the way inside and to her room.

Mother Grace escorted the silent Beth back to her room,
and called for Sister Agnes.

Agnes appeared and motioned Slocum into the kitchen,
where she bathed his cheek, then began to pull out splinters
with a pair of tweezers. "You had best go away and stay
away, Mr. Slocum," she said softly as she worked. "It
seems to me that you're nothing but a magnet for trouble."

Slocum replied, " 'Fraid I've got to agree with you on
that, Sister."

"Hold still," she said.

Mother Grace came down the hall and entered the
kitchen as well. "Will he live, Sister Agnes?"

"I'm afraid so."

"Tut tut, Sister," Mother Grace said, a smile on her lips
that reminded him of that little girl, long ago. And then she
turned her attention to Slocum. "Will more come?"

Slocum shook his head. "Doubt it. The sheriff only told
Donner, and he said Donner didn't stop at the telegrapher's
office on his way out of town. Too much of a rush, I'll wager. And Tanglewood doesn't leave his place, from what I
hear. At least, he doesn't go this far afield."

Mother Grace nodded. "We will pray that you are right,
Slocum."

"Yeah," he said, and grimaced when Sister Agnes pulled
out a particularly large splinter. "Me, too." He asked,
"What are you goin' to do with Beth?"

"Love her," said Mother Grace. "Make her at ease. Perhaps, one day, she will join our order. Or perhaps she will
be healed and go off to find a new life. We will do for her
what we can, and what God wishes."

"I kinda liked you better when you had dirt on your nose, and pigtails, and didn't talk so much about God, Mother Grace," he said with a grin.

Smiling, she patted him on the shoulder. "There, there, Slocum. You'll get used to me. Someday."

Bass Tanglewood was pissed, and that was putting it mildly. All day, and no word from that bastard, Donner! Hadn't he told the man to wire him at least twice a day? Hadn't he said he understood?

But here it was, a day and a half since Donner had wired from the Colorado River, and nothing—nothing!

It made him mad enough to bite nails, that's what it did.

He had gone up to Beth's room again to watch the sunset, but found that its bloody fingers only reminded him of her all the more, and so he had gone out to the south balcony off her room.

It had been a long time since he'd been out here. Probably a longer time since Beth had been out here, if ever. He kept all the keys, and the balcony doors were always locked. It was actually quite pleasant, he thought. You could just catch a whiff of the sea breeze. Not too much, though. Just right.

He walked to the railing at the far east end, where the sky was dark. East was where that little bitch, Beth, was. Stars were already rising in the skies. No, he corrected himself, becoming visible. They were there all the time, weren't they?

He leaned on the railing, noticing that it looked quite unkempt. The paint was peeling. And was that a spot of dry rot he saw? He made a mental note to get some of the men up here to paint it with a fresh coat of—

The rail gave way. Not quickly, it seemed to him, but in slow motion. Still, he was unable to catch himself. Too much of his weight had been over the rail as he leaned over it, to the east.

The fall seemed to take just as long. He thought about a pup he had owned when he was a boy, about the time his mother was killed by Pawnee, about a big stock deal he'd pulled off, and a hundred other things. And then he thought that he wouldn't die. No one died from falling just one story.

Unless they fell on their head.

He saw the rail of the hitching post rushing up to meet him.

He turned his head, but the movement came too late.

Bass Tanglewood was dead.

After a good week of high times with the delicious Rosie, Slocum's feet got to itching again. Word had just reached the Phoenix newspaper that Bass Tanglewood had passed away, the victim of a faulty porch rail.

Slocum had sent word up to Mother Grace that when Beth got to feeling better again—if she ever did—she could go home again. The danger was gone.

He went to the bank and deposited five thousand dollars in Rosie's account. He got quite a kick out of that. After all, he reasoned that he'd just toss it away on women and booze, or lose it in a card game. Better that it go to help somebody who'd make better use of it.

Rosie cried when he told her.

"Oh, Slocum." She sobbed. It seemed that was all she could say, because she just kept on repeating it, in between sniffling into his handkerchief and blowing her nose.

Slocum took her in his arms. "Rosie, honey, if I were you, I'd have the bank wire that money straight to a bank in San Francisco, and then I'd start writing letters to all the other places you've got your cash stashed, and tell them to do the same."

She nodded into his shoulder.

"And then I'd get the hell out of Phoenix just as fast as those kissable little feet of yours can carry you."

SLOCUM AND THE RUNAWAY BRIDE 187

She looked up, red-eyed but still beautiful. "There aren't any words, Slocum. Will I ever see you again, or are you gonna do the hero thing and ride off into the sunset?"

He chuckled. "Rosie, I promise you that the next time I'm in Frisco, I'll surely look you up. 'Course, you probably won't want to see an old saddle tramp like me, what with hobnobbin' with all those society folks . . ."

She burst into a new flood of waterworks. "Never!" She wept. "There'll never come a time when I won't want to see you!"

Slocum knew that money and prestige had surely changed a lot of people, but she was right. She wasn't one of them, and she wouldn't change.

He said, "All right, baby. Now it's time for me to go."

Slocum had held back quite a chunk of change for himself, too. He'd only spent about two hundred and some in Phoenix, and it had left him with thirty-eight hundred, plus the hundred pinned inside his vest, for emergencies. He figured to ride down to Tucson where things were a little more interesting, and the company was a little looser.

And there was always Conchita's Casa de Amour—an oddly named joint, if you asked him, but one that always offered a good time.

He thought that maybe he'd asked for Dory, first. She was a little redhead with a tight little ass and high, round breasts. Either that, or have a big plate of enchiladas at Mama Delores's place. Best enchiladas in all of Tucson, and that was saying something.

Grinning about Beth's good fortune—and Rosie's—and thoughts of Tucson and its mix of Mexican and Anglo and Indian people and foods, he rode on.

He just hoped Panther didn't catch sight of any pronghorn along the way.

Watch for

SLOCUM AND THE DEADWOOD DEAL

314th novel in the exciting SLOCUM series
from Jove

Coming in April!